STRAYING FROM THE PATH

STORIES FROM THE SOUR MAGIC SERIES OF FAIRY TALES

CHARITY TAHMASEB

COLLINS MARK BOOKS

COPYRIGHT

CONTENTS

LEAVING HOME

AN ARMY OF TOADS

A NEW PATH

HOW GOLDI LOST HER LOCKS

For Darcy

Until our paths cross again.

LEAVING HOME

WITH HAIR OF TEETH AND CLAW

SHE CAUGHT the thief with his hand wrapped around the stem of a flower, its spike of golden flocked petals sprouting from his fist. The brim of his hat shrouded his features, and the overcast night made it impossible to identify him. Even so, the witch knew a desperate husband when she encountered one.

"Let go of the lion's tail," she said, her words crisp as the air, with just enough bite to get her point across, but not so much that she didn't appear neighborly. She'd always been a good neighbor.

"My wife, Mistress Witch." The man sank to his knees. "She is with child."

"Yes. I know."

In truth, the entire village knew every time the babe kicked or the woman's back ached or her ankles swelled. Never had so many prayed for a timely birth.

"She craves all things fresh, all things green, all the things that grow in your garden. Please, Mistress. I will

3

work, split logs, do whatever you ask, but let me take some of your bounty home to her, so our babe might grow strong."

A first love, a first child, it was enough to make anyone a fool—or a thief. The witch spread her arms wide. "Take, neighbor. Take all that your wife craves." She grabbed hold of his hand. "Except for this."

Beneath her grip, he unclenched his fist. The plant he held—lion's tail, as the locals called it—dropped to the ground, stem broken, bright petals crushed.

"Leave the lion's tail," the witch said. "She should not eat it while with child, and I cannot be responsible for what happens if she does."

The man bowed, his movements jerky and frantic. The witch helped him pluck the best greens and place them in a basket. She saw him to the edge of her property, and when he hesitated, she urged him forward.

"Go," she said, voice gentle. "Take the greens and return to your wife."

When the man had left, the witch bent and plucked the lion's tail from the ground. She stroked the petals and wondered if his wife had already tasted of the plant.

That could be very bad indeed.

THE BABE WAS BORN STRONG, with a lusty cry and deep blue eyes that peered out at the world around her. Within a week, the entire village predicted she'd be a beauty. Within a month, her golden hair fell to her chin, the strands thick and wild. By nearly a year, the strands fought all attempts to comb them.

It was then that cries emerged from the cottage, by day and night, until the babe's mother ran from the house. Neighbors peered from their windows and did nothing, but the noise brought the witch from her garden.

The woman trembled, skirts in tatters, arms scratched. Blood oozed from wounds. In her hands, she clutched a pair of shears. She pointed the tip at the house and the infant inside.

"That is not my child. That cannot be my child."

She stood like that, her arm shaking, the shears more weapon than tool.

The witch examined the woman, gave a curt nod, then proceeded inside the cottage. Scattered strands of gold littered the floorboards from hearth to door. Other than a soft whimper, the room was quiet. She crouched to approach the babe.

"Shh … there you go. You are not in danger, and I will not hurt you." She gathered the child to her and stroked the remaining tufts of hair.

"See? I'm a friend. Let's find your mother."

The child cried out, fists clenched, but the witch hummed a lullaby, one with the power to sedate a charging troll. The babe blinked and then stared at the witch with curious blue eyes. The sight of them transfixed her, and the old witch's heart caught for a moment before resuming its natural beat. They stepped into the sunlight and into the crowd that now surrounded the cottage.

"She's the one!" the mother said, jabbing her shears

toward the witch. "She poisoned me with the plants from her garden."

"Your husband stole from my garden to satisfy your cravings."

The woman's hand shook, the tip of the shears bobbing. "That cannot be my child. She looks nothing like me."

Laughter rippled through the crowd. True, the woman was no beauty, and her husband no prince. The woman turned her wrath on the closest bystanders, silver shears glinting in the sunlight. The crowd eased back, catching laughter into cupped hands.

"Oh, then, perhaps the child is mine?" the witch asked.

This time, no one held back their laughter.

"So, you think I wasn't a beauty in my day?" The witch scanned the crowd, the babe still secured in one arm. "Master Tailor, I believe you know different."

The old man shuffled and stammered, a ruddy cast to his weathered cheeks. The witch turned back to the babe's mother.

"You do not want your child?" she said to the woman.

"That is not my child."

"Then, who will care for her?" The witch held the child aloft for the village to see. "No one, then?"

She considered the quiet bundle in her arms. A beauty, it was true, but those deep blue eyes were uncanny, knowing. No wonder this simple woman trembled at the sight of her own child.

The witch cast a look toward her own cottage and the

garden with its walls—ones that kept her tender plants safe from hooves and teeth. They kept the variety of weeds she cultivated from invading her neighbors' gardens. Walls were handy but not foolproof. Her gaze met the babe's, and once again, her heart caught.

In this case, perhaps she was the fool.

"I will care for her," the witch declared. "Please, before I take her with me, tell me her name."

The woman blinked as if waking from a dream. "She has no name."

"You have not named your child?" No wonder the babe lashed out. Even now, at the sound of the woman's voice, those short tufts of hair bristled, and the child cried out again.

"Oh, my poor child," the witch murmured. "Fate has been cruel."

No one stopped the witch from taking the child. No one uttered a word of protest. When the witch passed the mother so she might say goodbye, the woman only turned her back on both the witch and the child.

To the witch's surprise, the husband followed her home, weighed down by the cradle, a wee table, and a chair.

"Please, Mistress Witch, take these things for the child."

The witch nodded, held open the door to her cottage so the man might bring the items inside.

"Would you like to say goodbye before you leave?" she asked.

He had none of his wife's hesitation. His hand cupped

the babe's cheek. The tufts of hair wavered as if blown by a soft breeze, and the babe's eyes were luminous.

"Goodbye, sweet girl. Goodbye, my Rapunzel."

"Is that the child's name?" the witch asked.

"It is what I wanted to name her," he said, his voice wistful.

"Then, Rapunzel she'll be."

WITH RAPUNZEL still in the crook of her arm, the witch gazed about her cottage. Oh, it was a poor place to raise a child. Too many dried herbs that, consumed incorrectly, might injure or kill. Too many sharp objects. She inspected the child's head. Scars from the shears criss-crossed her raw scalp. Clearly, Rapunzel was no stranger to those.

She would need to find a grate for the hearth, a cow or goat for milking, soft cloth for diapers, and something other than the stained gown Rapunzel was wearing.

"It's been many years since I've even held a child," she said to the babe. "And I've never had any of my own."

At the thought, her heart caught once again. Had she ever intended to raise a child? Did she regret the time spent in the pursuit of her potions and spells? No. The village was a healthier, happier place for her efforts, even when its citizens didn't fully comprehend them.

"We can make do for now." The witch placed Rapunzel in her cradle. "I can soften bread in weak tea and stew some apples. Does that meet with your approval?"

Rapunzel sat up in her cradle, that unnerving blue-eyed stare never leaving the witch's face. Then the child clapped her hands together and gurgled.

"Well, I see that it does. Tomorrow, we will explore the village, get you some proper things. But tonight? Let's get to know one another."

It was late when Rapunzel fell asleep in the witch's arms. She eased her into the cradle only to be caught short by the babe's cries moments later.

She knelt at the cradle's side and cupped a hand against the child's soft cheek. "We both must get some rest."

The babe quieted immediately, but the moment the witch withdrew her hand, the cries started anew, stronger, more strident than before.

"Oh, very well. It has been a rough day."

She scooped the babe up and carried her to the large bed behind a curtained wall.

"I imagine you could use the comfort."

But when the witch extinguished the lamp and felt the babe curled at her side, tiny fingers clutching her thumb, she wondered which one of them truly needed the comfort.

IT WAS NOT the sudden acquisition of a child that shocked the witch. No, she'd come to terms with that during the darkest hours of the night. It was not the surprise of a cow tethered to the cottage gate. This, she suspected, was a gift from Master Tailor.

It was the way Rapunzel's hair had grown overnight. The strands curled and swirled. They felt like silk flowing through the witch's fingers, their length already to the child's chin.

The witch pulled ancient volumes from a shelf and thumbed through them, searching for something, anything that might tell her what manner of sorcery this was. She thought back to the man in her garden all those months ago. What had she given him?

She peered at the child who sat at her wee table. "Was it a combination of plants your mother ate?"

Rapunzel slapped the wood of the table, blue eyes stormy, hair undulating. It bristled, strands on end like those of a thistle.

"She is still your mother," the witch said, her voice soft but no-nonsense.

Another slap.

"Do you wish to be my daughter?"

Ah, the gurgle again. The hair calmed itself. Rapunzel peered at the witch, her blue eyes dark and serene.

"You shall be the daughter of my heart. Does that suit you?"

Rapunzel stood and toddled over to the witch. She clutched at her skirts with tiny fists.

"I see that it does." The witch bent down and pulled the child close. When she had Rapunzel nestled against her chest, the witch found herself stroking strands of that hair, much like she'd done all those months ago with the petals of the lion's tail. The locks slipped through her fingers as if they had a mind of their own.

"Inquisitive little beasts," she murmured.

And then froze. *The lion's tail.*

What manner of sorcery indeed.

"We have all been very, very foolish, I'm afraid," she whispered into the child's hair, "and you will be the one to pay for our folly."

THE WITCH TOOK Rapunzel with her everywhere. Aside from the father, there was no one she could trust in the village to watch the child and not gossip. And gossip they would. Already, rumors were flying about the miraculous growth of the child's hair.

Every morning, the witch worked to contain the strands before she left the house. In a bonnet. Secured with bows. The strands had a life of their own, flowing through her fingers, curling into points, flicking back and forth, very much like a tail.

"Until we reach the woods, child," the witch would say. "Contain them until we reach the woods."

Rapunzel blinked, a frown marring her little brow as if she were trying hard to comply.

Even with the babe in a sling, the witch felt lighter during her treks into the forest. At her age, she knew the senselessness of rushing. Leave that to the young. She'd complete her tasks all in good time. This morning was no different.

In a clearing, she set Rapunzel on a blanket, handed her a crust of bread to gnaw on, and began her work.

"I will teach you this," she said, flicking a glance and her words over one shoulder. "I will teach you which plants to consume and which ones to avoid. I'll show you when to cut, how to cut, and when neither of those things matters."

The witch inched her way around the clearing, always darting a look toward its center, toward Rapunzel. The child seemed content to chew her bread, clap her hands, and track the witch's progress. Not for the first time, the witch's thoughts drifted to Rapunzel's mother. How could she abandon such a child? So compliant. So calm.

"We will see how long that lasts, won't we?" the witch said with a wink.

Perhaps it was that steely gaze, or the miracle of the hair that now hid the scars on Rapunzel's scalp, but the witch swore the child understood more than she ought.

"Which makes me feel less foolish when I talk to myself," she added.

Rapunzel gurgled.

The witch was near the old willow tree when a cry sounded behind her. Her throat tightened, and she was certain some harm had come to Rapunzel. Or perhaps the mother had a change of heart, had followed them this morning, and was intent on stealing the child away.

Instead, when she turned, the witch came nose to nose

with a river rat. The thing was large and hairy, its gray fur matted and stinking of stagnant water. This was not the sort of creature that kept the barn cats fat. This was the sort of creature that took whiskers and tails as trophies.

Where there was one rat, there would be another; they hunted in pairs. She'd survive a bite, although the infection would linger, and nastily so. Rapunzel? The daughter of her heart? A child barely bigger than a cat?

The cry went up again. The witch started forward, taking an inventory of the arsenal she had on hand. A pair of shears. Some twine. A handful of willow branches that she might fashion into a switch.

Rapunzel was still sitting in the center of the clearing. Despite the tears that washed her cheeks and the tiny hands clenched into fists, she was unharmed. It was the sight of the child's hair that froze the witch in place.

The strands had grown, not by inches, but whole yards. They flowed across the clearing as if exploring new territory. They curled and lashed out, the ends sharpening into points. Like teeth. Like claws.

Several locks had already trapped the second rat, bound it neck to tail, so all the witch could see of it was its grubby nose and crooked whiskers. Now, several locks worked in tandem, approaching the first rat from two sides and from behind. The creature hissed—at the witch, at its predicament. A predator such as this always knew when it had met its match.

It made one desperate lunge, an attempt to inflict injury before succumbing itself. Claws extended, teeth bared, it launched itself from the branch, its target the witch's face.

The golden strands of Rapunzel's hair caught the beast midair. A slashing. A slicing. The carcass tumbled to the ground and landed with a soft thud.

Only for a moment did the witch hesitate. Only for a moment did she consider what the villagers might make of this child. Cries of *monster* echoed in the back of her mind. But then she rushed to the center of the clearing. The golden strands parted, let the witch through to her child, and she clutched Rapunzel to her.

With that tender embrace and her quiet words, the hair relaxed its guard. The strands softened their points and retracted until their length was a touch longer than earlier that day.

The witch cupped Rapunzel's face. "Do you know what it is you can do, child?"

Rapunzel stared, unblinking.

"Is it even you who is doing this, or is it your wonderfully monstrous hair?"

At those words, the strands extended, a lock wrapping around the witch's wrist, none too gently.

"Cut that out," she said to the golden rope around her wrist. "It takes offense far too quickly. We will have to work on that."

The hair tightened its grasp while a separate lock flicked back and forth, once again an angry tail.

"If you are to live in this world, you will need to learn to control your hair."

Rapunzel stared back, steely-eyed as ever. Then she clapped her hands together and gurgled.

The hair relaxed its grip and flowed into golden ringlets.

The witch released a sigh. Yes, to live in this world. That would not be an easy thing.

RAPUNZEL SOON OUTGREW her cradle and wee table and chair. Her hair evaded all attempts to tame or trim it, and the strands quickly traveled down her back past her knees until they swept the ground. Every morning, the witch would braid the strands, and Rapunzel would loop the plaits around her arms or her waist. She grew into her beauty and her strength, for she did everything under the weight of her hair.

The witch became deft at avoiding the majority of the villagers who might cause problems. The father was kind and no worry. He left Rapunzel all manner of carvings and trinkets. Master Tailor kept them in cow's milk, although the witch made a point to avoid his wife.

Once, on a walk to the forest, they encountered Rapunzel's mother. The woman was herding two children —twins—in front of her. The girls were dancing along the lane, skinny arms freckled, red hair thin but flowing down their backs—free of all of the constraints the witch placed on Rapunzel's hair.

The daughter of her heart halted, her spine impossibly straight beneath the weight of all her hair. She locked her gaze on the trio, strands of hair straining against their braids.

Then one lock escaped, slithered down the lane after the mother and the two girls. A few strands wrapped themselves around the woman's ankle. It was then that the witch pulled the shears from her apron pocket and snipped the lock.

The strands released their grip, twitched much like a dying snake, and at last ceased all movement. The woman walked on, oblivious.

"She cannot hurt you, child," the witch said.

Rapunzel glared, a non-answer if there ever was one. She was at that age—no longer a true child, not yet a woman. And the witch knew she'd spoken a lie.

Of course the mother still had the power to hurt. All mothers did. Try as she might, the witch couldn't banish the image of the quivering strands of hair lying along the dusty lane. Try as she might, she couldn't muster the courage to ask for forgiveness.

But that night, Rapunzel crept into the witch's bed, curled next to her, and clutched her thumb with long, slender fingers.

ONE MORNING in Rapunzel's sixteenth year, they awoke to an odd humming that came from outside the cottage. Rapunzel peered through the shutters, her hands poised to open them to the morning sunshine, her fingers unmoving.

"Child, please, let in the fresh air," the witch said.

Rapunzel's hands remained still. "There are many strange men outside our door."

On the way to the door, the witch secured a broom. She sprang across the threshold, broom handle connecting with a jaw here, a temple there.

"Go, go! All of you. She is too young to marry."

True, Rapunzel had fully grown into her beauty, and when tame, her hair was a sight to behold, glimmering without the benefit of light. The witch had not anticipated this, however. Not so soon, and not so many suitors.

In retrospect, perhaps she should have.

Rapunzel's father took to guarding the path to the cottage, but this only worked for so long. Men came daily, hourly, knocks on the door, the windows. More than one man tried the chimney, only to find his breeches smoldering from a stoked fire.

After a night of off-key serenading that had left them both bleary-eyed, the witch decided.

"We must leave the village."

The daughter of her heart peered through the shutters, the tips of her braids twitching. "Why do they want me? They do not even know me."

"They want your beauty."

"But my beauty isn't me. If that is all they want, then surely I will disappoint them."

"That is something none of them understand."

Rapunzel's gaze darted toward the door. Already a fresh crop of men had lined the path, their murmurs rising in the morning air.

"But how?" she asked. "How will we leave?"

"Do they make you angry?"

"Oh, they do."

"Remember that when you step outside, and all will be well."

Rapunzel's father packed the wagon and hitched the horses. For the first time since the day he had given his daughter away, he ventured inside the witch's cottage, cupped her cheek, and told her goodbye forever.

The witch stepped from her cottage for the last time, the cries and calls of the men thickening the air around her.

"Going somewhere, Mistress Witch?"

"Can we follow?"

"Is there room in your wagon for me?"

Men lined the path three deep. The witch traveled its center until she reached the wagon. There, she climbed into the driver's seat and took the reins from Rapunzel's father. She gave him a reassuring nod before speaking to the men who had chased her from her home.

"Gentlemen," she said, "if I were you, I'd step back."

No one heeded her warning.

When Rapunzel emerged, the cries grew louder still. Jeering and whistles and bids for attention. One man and then another blocked her path. Two grabbed her wrists. A third—the tallest and fairest, the only one dressed in nobleman's attire—pushed the others aside in his quest for her.

But when the last of her unencumbered hair cleared the

doorway, a gasp filled the air. The strands whipped and whirled, the ends sharpening into teeth, into claws. The men released her. Some ran, the nobleman among them. Others froze in place. Rapunzel walked, expression serene, hands folded in front of her, while her hair dispatched the men.

The slate walkway ran with blood. Bits of flesh speckled the walls of the witch's garden. The cries went from jeering to unearthly, the agony sharp in the air.

No one followed them from the village.

THEY RODE FOR DAYS, stopping only to sleep. The first night, when Rapunzel wished to keep them dry from the rain, her hair wove itself into a shelter.

"Oh, it can shield as well," Rapunzel said, her fingers investigating the crosshatch of strands above their heads, her eyes curious once again.

"Indeed it can, my child. Indeed it can."

At last they came to the borderlands, to a stone watchtower long abandoned. The space around it was vast and empty—only hill after hill that stretched toward the horizon. No sign of a village, a farm, or even a hunter's cabin. Desolate and barren and the perfect spot for the two of them.

"Here," the witch said. "We can make this our home."

And yet, even as she said these words, the ground shook with the force of approaching horses. In the distance, the standard of the war prince fluttered above a line of soldiers on horseback.

"Quick, Rapunzel, hide. In the wagon. Pull in all your hair."

The wagon creaked with the weight of Rapunzel and all her hair. The horses whinnied as if they wished to cover the sound. They were good beasts, the witch thought, and they loved Rapunzel almost as much as she did.

When the war prince arrived, the witch bowed low.

"Mistress Witch, may I ask what you're about?" the prince said.

He was a powerful man, large and dark, a mask partially shrouding his features. His eyes, black and inquisitive, took in everything. They surveyed the tower, the horses, the wagon, all before returning to the witch.

"But of course, Your Highness," the witch said. "I plan to use this tower for my home. It is no longer in your use, is that right?"

"That's true, but the borderlands are dangerous, and my army is small in number." He waved a hand at the group behind him. They were a motley crew, large and small, green-skinned or not, pockmarked or masked for reasons the witch decided not to contemplate.

"I cannot guarantee your protection," he added.

"And I do not ask for it. All I ask for is quiet to practice my craft."

"And if a troll happens by while you're practicing your craft?" Now, those dark eyes were lit with humor.

"Oh, Your Highness, I have lived long enough to know exactly what to do with a troll if one happens by."

The prince laughed. "I believe you do, Mistress Witch. But be warned, this is a lonely stretch of land. Men seldom travel it."

"That's what makes it perfect, Your Highness."

He laughed again, as if he took her meaning. He bade her farewell and rode away, his soldiers following, their horses kicking up dust that floated on the humid air. The witch tasted that air and licked her lips.

"It will rain soon," she declared. "Let's get settled."

The watchtower had a single entrance that the witch sealed over once their belongings were inside. It was cozy here, space enough to work and live, and the window let in sunlight and fresh air but would shield them from rain.

"But how will we leave?" Rapunzel asked.

"I will climb down the face of the tower," the witch said. "There are hand and footholds that should not crumble beneath my weight. Or perhaps your clever hair might weave itself into a ladder."

At the suggestion, the golden strands did just that, the construction so quick it produced a breeze within the circular room.

"But I cannot climb down a ladder of my own hair," Rapunzel began, then clamped her mouth shut. "Oh, I see. This is to be my prison."

"Not a prison, child, but a sanctuary." The witch laid her palm against Rapunzel's cheek. "If your hair were not so fierce, so untamable, you might seek a quiet life in some faraway village. But when we left, your hair felled two dozen strong men."

"And no one wants to live near a monster."

The witch tugged her close, wrapping her bony arms around the daughter of her heart. "You are no monster."

"But my hair—"

"Seeks out injustice. It always has. Why would it attack the woman who gave you life, but not your father? Why does it lash out at men whose only interest is your beauty?"

"The world doesn't want that sort of justice, does it?"

"I'm afraid it does not."

"I shall stay, then." Rapunzel gathered handfuls of her hair. It flowed and swayed and cascaded to the floor in waves. "We shall stay. Perhaps I can teach it to behave."

The witch spent her days in the forest, gathering herbs and berries. Every fortnight, she ventured to the nearest village for supplies. She traded with merchants there, weaving her deception. Just an old crone brewing potions and remedies. That spring, the lion's tail grew thick in the woods. Every time the witch caught sight of it, she flinched, only to confront yet another clump a few feet away.

Rapunzel practiced remedies and potions along with the witch. Together, they cultivated containers of herbs and small plants so Rapunzel might feel the soil beneath her fingers without leaving the tower. Beneath her touch, the plants flourished. She coaxed all manner of exotic flowers from the soil, even those the witch had never managed to on her own. Their petals brightened the little room and perfumed the air.

At night, she studied history and took a particular interest in the battles once waged in the borderlands and the ghosts said to walk and howl, searching for their old regiments or gutted homes.

"I do not hear these howls," Rapunzel said one evening. She lifted the heavy locks that lay beneath her hands. "Perhaps my hair is too thick against my ears."

"Perhaps people search for excuses not to inhabit these lands," the witch said.

"Perhaps." Rapunzel remained at the window for a long time, her gaze exploring the borderlands, the tips of her hair twitching like that of a penned beast.

For eight months, they lived in quiet in their watch-tower. The war prince had been right. Few strayed this close to the border. Once, the prince himself rode by on patrol, a small group of soldiers at his side.

"I see you live well, Mistress Witch," he called out.

The witch leaned from the tower's window and called back, "Very well and very alone, Your Highness. However, I see you have added to your party."

The witch inclined her head as the prince's younger brother rode forward. He was light where the war prince was dark, unmasked and unscarred. Even from a distance, the witch felt those legendary gray eyes taking in every-thing. In this, he was very much like his brother.

With a hand, she shielded her own eyes and hid her frown. There was something about him that unsettled her. True, she never paid much heed to palace gossip. Even so, she knew that the younger prince preferred the boudoir to the battlefield for his conquests.

With as much stealth as possible, she gestured at Rapunzel, urging the child to conceal herself further, to constrain every last strand of golden hair. Rapunzel merely covered her mouth with a hand so as to not to laugh out loud, her hair rippling across the floor with repressed mirth.

"Perhaps this stretch of land is not so lonely for you now, Your Highness," the witch said, her voice rougher than she liked.

The war prince cast his brother a look. "Perhaps not."

As the party rode off, the witch considered that perhaps she and the war prince also had something in common.

They were both liars.

LATER, the witch would admit that she'd grown complacent. Life with the daughter of her heart was more than she had ever hoped for. Her trips to the village grew more frequent. Perhaps those gave her away. Perhaps she called too loudly for Rapunzel to lower her ladder of hair. Perhaps someone followed her and spied on them, although who would be curious about an old crone living alone, the witch couldn't say.

But when she returned from her most recent trip to the village and saw not the golden ladder of hair but one of wood propped against the tower, the witch knew she'd betrayed Rapunzel in some fashion. She dropped the reins and leaped from the wagon. The horse, so gentle and loving, simply continued forward to meet its sister. The witch scampered up the ladder, her hands catching on the rough grain so much that she had to claw her way to the window.

There, in the center of the room, Rapunzel stood. Around her, strands of her hair whipped and whirled, the ends sharp and deadly. Like teeth. Like claws. A monster of a thing. On the floor? A man.

A dead man—a dead nobleman, from the looks of his clothes—one who had suffered the death of a thousand cuts, a thousand bites. One whose breeches were around his ankles. One whose hand had torn away the bodice of Rapunzel's dress.

"He surprised me. I never heard him until he had cleared the window." Rapunzel stared straight ahead, her gaze on the window, not on the man, and not on the witch, a hollow look haunting her blue eyes. "And then … and then … Mother, I'm … I'm …"

"No!" Although flight had never been one of the witch's skills, she flew across the room, cradled Rapunzel to her. "You are not sorry. This is not your fault."

"But—"

"He is dead. A lone nobleman, venturing out on his own, in the borderlands? This will surprise no one."

"Turn him," Rapunzel said, her voice devoid of emotion, a dead thing.

Panic gripped the witch, had her by the throat. With a foot, she complied, heaving the dead man onto his back.

Fair hair. Royal crest.

The war prince's brother.

"He will come searching, won't he?" Rapunzel said. This was no question. "The war prince will search for his brother."

"Perhaps. The borderlands are vast. It may be months before we see him again. And by then?" The witch surveyed the man, the window, and considered how they might accomplish this next task.

"If your hair can lower him to the ground, I shall bury him in the woods. I feel winter in my bones. An early snowfall will be welcome."

Rapunzel nodded. "I shall scrub his blood from our floor."

Without another word, Rapunzel's hair wrapped the man from head to foot and lifted him through the tower's window, then lowered him to the earth. When the witch reached the ground, she was surprised to find the longest strands of hair in a dense copse behind the tower, the claws already digging a grave.

By the time the witch found a shovel, the man was deep in the ground. So she took up an ax and splintered the ladder into kindling. And by the time she finished that chore, those beastly strands of hair had scattered dry leaves across the grave, the fresh-turned soil all but hidden.

She eased a hand beneath a lock of that hair. "Thank you," she said. "Thank you for protecting her. Thank you for being so fierce."

The strands wrapped and unwrapped themselves

around her wrist before caressing her cheek.

DESPITE HER OWN WORDS, the witch knew. A dead prince was still a dead prince, and justice would be served. A week later, when the war prince rode up with a contingent of his soldiers, she was ready to face that justice.

"Good day to you, Mistress Witch."

The witch was standing at the base of the tower. "And to you, Your Highness." She bowed low. She liked this dark and masked prince, even though today he would, no doubt, declare her death sentence.

"I wonder if you can help me."

"I will try, Your Highness."

"My brother has gone missing. You met him on our last patrol through these parts. Did you happen to see him or even converse with him?"

Behind the prince, one of his soldiers unleashed a dog. Oh, yes, the witch thought, he knew the answer already. A moment later, so did everyone else. The hound let out a howl before digging at the fresh grave.

"Tell me, Mistress Witch, how did he come to die?"

She drew herself up tall, raised her chin. "I killed him, Your Highness."

To her surprise, the prince laughed—a dark, somber laugh, to be sure, but a laugh, nevertheless. "I doubt that."

"Doubt what you will, Your Highness, but do you see anyone else here?"

"You have just admitted to murder, and of one of the royal family. Do you wish for death?"

"I am but an old crone, and death does not scare me."

"I suspect you might scare death itself," the prince murmured. "But you leave me no choice." With a sigh, he addressed the soldier next to him. "Arrest her." He returned his attention to the witch. "Unless you can give me a compelling reason not to."

"I can give you that reason."

The voice came from above, and it rang high and clear and unimpeded over the borderlands. The witch whirled, her chest constricting. No. Not Rapunzel. *No.* She shook her head, but the daughter of her heart paid her no heed.

Without another word, Rapunzel stepped onto the window's ledge. She jumped, her hair fanning out behind her before rushing to the ground to cushion her fall. She landed on her feet, knee-deep in golden locks.

"Your Highness, no," the witch began. "Please listen. She—"

The prince held up a hand, silencing her. "Let her speak."

"I killed him, Your Highness," Rapunzel said.

"Did you, now? And you are?"

"Rapunzel."

"Rapunzel? With hair of teeth and claw?"

"I … Is that what they call me?"

"You are but a legend, a whispered story. I—" He broke off, his gaze drawn to the woods where the younger prince was buried. "My brother spoke of you."

"I am very real, Your Highness, and I have killed your brother."

"You confess to murder, then?"

"In self-defense, but yes, I do."

The prince fell silent. The soldiers behind him shifted in their saddles. The one who managed the dog corralled and leashed the beast. Then, with a single, deliberate motion, the prince removed the black leather mask to reveal a face crisscrossed with scars.

"Look upon this face, Rapunzel," he commanded.

And she did.

"I have lost my only brother."

"I am sorry for your loss, Your Highness."

"You must understand that yes, he was my brother, and I confess to loving the boy he once was, but not the man he became." The prince contemplated Rapunzel as he spoke, as if taking in her full measure, as if sizing up an opponent. "That, perhaps, was unfair of me, unfair to him."

The prince drew his sword, the metal blade singing out. He aimed the blow directly at Rapunzel. A cry lodged in the witch's throat, and it took all her strength not to sink to her knees.

Rapunzel's hair whipped and whirled. When the frenzy subsided, she and the prince were standing mere feet from each other, the tip of his sword poised at the hollow of her throat, the claws of her hair wrapped around his neck.

His soldiers sprang forward, weapons drawn.

"Stand down!" the prince called. When no one

moved, he sheathed his sword and said, "Stand down. She doesn't intend to injure me."

"True. I don't." With Rapunzel's words, her hair unraveled from around the prince's neck.

"And why is that?" He rubbed the skin of his throat, the move born of curiosity rather than pain.

"You did not intend to hurt me."

"And your hair." He gestured to the locks undulating along her back and on the ground. "It knew that."

"Yes, Your Highness."

A smile lit the prince's scarred face, then a laugh made it almost handsome. "Then I am lucky, for that was only my guess." This time when he contemplated Rapunzel, his gaze was lit with interest. "And now I face another sort of dilemma, for I have not only lost my brother but my best fighter."

The witch's heart caught. The tips of her fingers grew cold, her legs numb. "Your Highness, you can't possibly mean—"

Once again, the prince silenced the witch's protest with the barest flick of his wrist.

"I mean everything I say, Mistress Witch." He directed his gaze toward Rapunzel once again. "Will you join my company and replace the man you have killed?"

Murmurs rose from the assembled soldiers. One stepped forward and probed a lock of hair with the toe of his boot. The strands curled around his ankle, and the man landed on the ground.

"She is but a girl!" another called out.

"I am strong," Rapunzel said. She hefted her hair in

both her hands. "I have been carrying the weight of this all my life."

"A burden, indeed," the prince said.

"How will she ride?" someone else asked. "We have no cart for all that hair. We travel light."

Before the soldier had even stopped speaking, her hair swirled. It wove complicated patterns, fitting itself to her body until she was covered in what looked like golden chainmail.

"It seems I won't need any armor," Rapunzel said. "Or a cart."

"Any more dissent? Perhaps you'd like to confer with my brother." The prince gestured at the grave. "I'm certain he has an opinion."

With the prince's words, the witch knew the matter was settled. Strength returned to her limbs, and a strange, detached determination filled her. She saddled a horse, and the sisters whinnied their goodbyes, tails swishing. She secured a bag of provisions and one of potions and remedies. If she could, the witch would have packed her heart as well, for it was too swollen and sore in her own chest.

"Goodbye, daughter of my heart." The witch presented the reins to Rapunzel.

"Mother?" Rapunzel's eyes grew large, as if she was only now realizing the consequences of her choice. "I don't want—"

The witch hushed her. "Of course you do. It is right and good for children to leave home, to have adventures. This prince is a good man," she added. "He will not lead you astray."

"I can't promise you comfort," the prince added. "Or even safety. But adventure? That, I can promise."

Rapunzel's gaze went once again to the horizon, her eyes lit with the promise of adventure that it held.

"Go with him, child. Go and be free."

Rapunzel hugged the witch, mounted her horse, and joined the prince's company. They rode off, and the witch tracked them until Rapunzel had blended into the horizon. Even then, the witch stood at the base of the tower. At last, she turned and confronted its surface.

"I'm not sure I know the spell to conjure up another entrance, or a staircase, for that matter." She said these words to the horse, who snuffled and snorted a reply. "I'm not sure these old bones can stand the climb."

Before the witch could even try, a golden ladder tumbled from the window. She grasped the silky strands, hardly daring to breathe, and climbed up to the ledge. Once she was standing inside, the strands returned to the tower. They flowed through the window and into one of Rapunzel's containers of exotic flowers, where they burrowed beneath the soil.

Then, in a moment that was no more than a blink of an eye, a stem pushed up and through, and the bloom of a lion's tail unfurled.

FIRST PUBLISHED in The Shapeshifter Chronicles in July 2016 by Windrift Books.

A MOST MARVELOUS PAIR OF BOOTS

It was during the wedding feast, when the air was heavy with roast goose and red wine, that Mirabella realized they'd all been duped by a cat.

Her new husband, the Marquis of Carabas, was sitting to her right, his teeth tearing goose flesh, grease coating his lips. She shuddered and pushed away thoughts of the marriage bed. Her father, the king, was well into his cups and tore at his food as if to mimic his new son-in-law. He slapped the marquis on the back and praised heaven that—at long last—Mirabella had found herself a husband.

At long last, indeed.

Near the end of the table, the cat was lounging, booted hind legs crossed. With a paw, he wiped goose fat from his whiskers. Mirabella fixed her gaze on him until he raised his yellow eyes and took in her full measure.

Then, the creature winked.

She sat back, a flush heating her cheeks, traveling her

neck, and ending somewhere near her décolletage. She sighed, not in the mood for wine, song, or her new husband. True, the marquis was handsome. A point in his favor, to be sure. A goose leg slipped through his fingers, and he stopped its descent with one meaty hand. Mirabella cringed and again shoved thoughts of the marriage bed from her mind.

She turned to her new husband and asked, "More wine?"

Without waiting for an answer, she filled his goblet to the rim. He'd barely spoken since they'd exchanged *I do.* Come to think of it, the lad—for he was hardly older than she—seldom spoke more than a word or two at a time. Mirabella leaned forward and, once again, trained her gaze on the cat. This time when he winked, she didn't flinch.

Oh, there was no Marquis of Carabas. She's stake her somewhat tarnished reputation on it. Certainly, if this lad were nobility, he would've curried her father's favor long before now. Not only that, but he was untouched by palace gossip, which was rife with rumors about her improper relationship with her tutor. In her defense, the relationship hadn't been at all improper.

Well, maybe a little bit improper.

But thanks to some rumors and a fast-talking cat, her father was now praising the heavens and had shoved this lad into her arms and her bed. Would he care to know the truth about the marquis? Of course not. A married daughter was one less burden, especially a daughter with a somewhat tarnished reputation.

The splash of wine against her chest forced a gasp from her. The red liquid soaked into the bodice of her gown, the spot resembling a sword wound. Her new husband stared at his empty goblet as if the wine had sprung forth of its own accord. Her father pounded the marquis on the back, his hearty laugh filling the banquet hall. And, at the end of the table, that damn cat winked.

HER NEW HUSBAND'S snores filled the bedchamber. From her vantage point on the balcony, Mirabella could see the outline of his form on the duvet. Make no mistake, it was a fine form, despite the drool.

"You admire my master, then, Princess?"

Ah, that damn cat.

"There is more to admire in a man than form or face, Master Cat."

The cat trod along the balcony's edge, feet whisper-soft against the stone, even with the boots.

"What is it you wish?" he said.

"I fear my wishes matter not to man or cat."

"I did not ask that."

Mirabella glanced into the bedchamber. Yes, assuredly, her new husband would not wake until noon, if then. "Tonight's wish has already been granted."

Could cats grin? Well, this one could, and did, twirling long whiskers with a paw. "And tomorrow's wish?"

Yes, the crux of the matter.

"I cannot simply un-marry, Master Cat, and I doubt my new husband will appreciate his rival." She gestured toward the telescope at the balcony's far end. She had yet to peer at the night sky this evening—or rather, morning. Of course, at this moment, the only view was of a cat's tail, which was swishing in front of the lens.

Still, the urge to lean over the telescope remained. For a few hours, she could pretend that Sebastian was still at her side, imagine his fingers lighting on the back of her neck, hear his ardent whisper. "Do you see it?"

The night spent with her tutor fueled court gossip even now. That the two of them had gazed at the stars and not into each other's eyes was of little matter. As she ran a hand along the telescope, the skies were clear, but her mind was clouded with thoughts of the upcoming tour of the kingdom. The grand celebration of her marriage meant visiting people she didn't much care for and receiving gifts she certainly didn't need. But the real question was: pack the telescope or leave it behind?

"You'll be traveling light," the cat said.

"Unlikely, Master Cat. Have you never seen a royal entourage take to the roads?"

"I have, Princess. It's all part of the plan."

"What plan is that?"

"Do you not wish to see your Sebastian again?"

Her hand stilled on the telescope, her fingers ice. Damn palace gossip, and damn that cat besides. How could he know her heart?

"You keep a great many unsent letters beneath your bed."

Oh. That was how.

"Would you like to be free? Study with your tutor in peace?"

Mouth dry, Mirabella nodded.

"Then, trust me."

"I shall do no such thing, Master Cat."

"But what if you could un-marry, Princess?" the cat asked. "Would you trust me then?"

"What God has joined together, let no man put asunder," Mirabella replied. "Even cats know this."

Ah, yes, cats could grin. "Oh, Princess, have you not noticed? I am certainly no man."

THE CARRIAGE BUMPED OVER NEVER-ENDING ruts. A week on the road, and the only sign of the cat had been this morning, when he had slipped a wineskin into Mirabella's hands.

"Hold it beneath your cloak," he said. "Just so."

Only thoughts of her studies, of Sebastian, compelled her to comply. She cradled her burden and settled in for another long day.

A cry rose up outside the carriage.

"Brigands!" a guard shouted.

Swords clanked, and then the carriage door flew open. The cat sprang past her, a single claw piercing the wineskin. Red bloomed beneath her hand, the wine soaking her gown. The marquis took one look at the stain spreading across her bodice and crashed to the carriage floor, face-first. Never mind that she reeked of her father's finest vintage (come to think of it, so did the marquis); she was, in everyone's view, fatally wounded.

And with death came freedom. Un-marry, indeed.

Before she could leap from the carriage, a paw tugged on her sleeve.

"You'll need this, Princess." The cat proffered a dusty cloak, ragged along the hem. He dropped a small canvas sack at her feet. "And of course, you'll need these." He pulled the boots from his hind legs.

He crouched, then sprang through the carriage window, and Mirabella swore his final sentence was more caterwaul than words. She pulled on the boots, the leather kissing her legs, the soles cupping her feet. She held one leg extended, turning it to study the boot. How was this possible?

No matter. They fit. She jumped from the carriage. The boots carried her through sword clashes and rearing horses. No one called out. No one stopped her. Except for a cat that wove between her ankles.

"Master Cat?"

His tail twitched, and he blinked slowly, but that was all.

She nestled him in her arms, the cloak shielding them both, and took to the road.

That night, she tugged the boots from her feet and placed them far enough from her campfire that no spark would reach them.

"Master Cat, would you like to take a turn in your boots?"

Within moments, the cat was standing before her in all his booted glory. He surveyed their surroundings.

"Seems safe enough," he said. "I shall fetch dinner and return shortly."

Mirabella pointed to the pot simmering over the fire. "I have dinner."

"I shall fetch us a decent dinner, then."

She huffed but couldn't argue. Her skills with a telescope far surpassed anything she could manage with a cook pot.

"I shall almost regret finding Sebastian," she said to him later, over stew and a loaf of hard crusted bread from a nearby village. "I will miss these marvelous boots."

"Why not commission another pair?" the cat asked, strutting about, the leather boots glowing warmly in the light of the fire.

"How will I do that, Master Cat? I will be a scholar, and a somewhat impoverished one at that."

"Haven't you guessed, Princess? Who do you think gave me these boots to begin with?"

"Not the marquis?"

"Hardly."

"But then—"

"Princess, you know their creator. Intimately, if I dare say so."

"But ... Sebastian is a scholar. He studies—"

"The mysteries of our world—and he has mastered a few."

Mirabella sucked in a breath and blew out a stream of

air rather than harsh words. After all, what was there to say?

With a paw, the cat twirled his whiskers, and then strode off into the night. So, it had been Sebastian all along.

And, of course, that damn cat.

FIRST PUBLISHED IN TIMELESS TALES, January 2014

AN ARMY OF TOADS

CHAPTER 1

FOR GEMMA, the worst part about being swept from her own home was not the sharp smack of the broom across her backside or the fact that it was her mother doing the sweeping and the smacking.

It was the dust that clogged the air in the wake of both. Dust that filled her nose and coated her lips, dust that choked her. When she landed on the worn path in front of her home and her palms struck the earth, that dust billowed once again. Gemma let out a cry.

And from her mouth fell three tiny toads.

Her mother screamed, her anger renewed. "Worthless! Worthless girl! One simple request, and you can't even accomplish that. How difficult is it to give an old crone a sip of water?"

Old crone? Or had it been a fine lady who had crossed her path? Not that it mattered. She'd seen through the trick almost immediately. The task itself hadn't been difficult at all, but that wasn't the point.

There was no use explaining how she had refused the old woman's gift. Her mother wouldn't listen.

The shadow of the broom stretched across the path, and the tiny toads scampered away. Her wrists ached, the backs of her legs stung, and the dust continued its onslaught. Gemma swallowed her cries, her words—any sound that might produce more toads—and braced for the blow.

"Madam, I command you to stop!" The voice was strong, confident, *royal*.

The broom's shadow wavered, then vanished. Gemma remained on her hands and knees.

"You're distressing my beloved," the man continued.

"Please, Mother, stop. Gemma has done nothing wrong." With her sister's words came the plink of diamonds falling from her mouth.

The broom smacked the earth rather than the backs of Gemma's legs. Their mother rushed forward, grasping for the gemstones as if the ground itself might steal them from her.

Gemma sat back on her heels and planted her sore palms against her thighs. Only now did she notice the carriage, its trim gilded, its interior lush with velvet. The man was trimmed similarly, in midnight velvet and gold braid.

So Rose's prince did exist. Handsome. Of course he was. Princes always were, it seemed. No doubt he would spirit her sister away—to somewhere better, Gemma hoped. He extended a hand to help Rose from the carriage. Then he turned his attention to Gemma and offered her that same hand.

She glanced at her soiled hands and—to save them both the embarrassment—stood on her own, shook the dust from her skirt, and bobbed a curtsy in thanks.

Their mother searched the path and the area around Rose for any wayward gems. It was as if the woman had forgotten everything else, fingers and eyes greedy for the diamonds. Gemma barely recognized the woman their mother had become, but that had started long before Rose came home spitting gemstones.

If Gemma had to pick one day when everything had changed, it wouldn't have been the day their father had died. Rather, it was a week after the funeral, when their mother had walked into the forest and didn't emerge for three days.

What had happened to her there, no one knew. Some said the magic had soured and it was foolhardy to stray into the enchanted forest. Perhaps it was grief. Whatever the case, the woman was now cradling the diamonds close to her breast the way she had once held her children.

"Mother, I am leaving." Rose held out her hands as she spoke so when the precious stones slipped from her mouth, they fell into her palms. "These should keep you quite comfortable."

Rose's cupped hands overflowed with all manner of stones—rubies and sapphires, emeralds, and of course, diamonds. They glinted in the sunlight, casting Rose in an ethereal glow.

"Oh, my dear girl! You are too generous." The woman lunged for the treasure.

Rose pulled her hands away. "I don't want you harming Gemma."

"But of course not! I love both my daughters equally."

Gemma barely swallowed back the snort. For a moment, she felt a lump, as if a frog had lodged itself in her throat.

"And she may stay here if she wishes."

Their mother's mouth puckered. Her eyes grew flinty. "But of course."

Gemma shook her head. She'd take her chances in the enchanted forest before she spent another night under her mother's roof.

"Are you certain?" Rose turned to her now, blue eyes soft with concern.

Gemma nodded. The sight of her mother's gaze, still flinty, had told her all she needed to know.

"Allow Gemma inside to gather her things." Rose's command came with another three diamonds.

Without waiting for her mother's consent, Gemma rushed into the cottage. Her belongings were meager, true, but if she were to venture out on her own, she'd need the sturdy pair of leather boots, her cloak, the knife and scabbard her father had given her. She tugged on the boots, secured everything else into a bedroll, and slung that over her shoulder.

Outside, Rose had spoken a king's treasure for their mother. The woman gazed at the stones lovingly, fingers stroking their facets. The gems sparkled, but it was a harsh, icy sort of light, and it made their mother look gray and sickly.

Gemma wanted to warn her. All the diamonds in the world would not keep her warm. But there was no use in talking, not anymore.

Rose took Gemma by the hands and drew her to the rear of the carriage.

"Oh, Gemma, I wish I understood why..." Her words were no more than whispers, laced with tears. Tiny seed pearls slipped from her mouth and into the pocket of Gemma's apron.

How could she explain to Rose when she could barely explain to herself? Something—her own contrary nature, perhaps—had made her refuse the crone's gift. Now, here she was, cursed instead.

That had not been one of Gemma's wiser decisions.

"Are you certain you won't come with us?"

More seed pearls fell until Gemma's pockets were bulging with them.

"Giles wouldn't mind." Rose cast an adoring look at her prince. "Once we arrive, surely the king won't, either."

Oh, surely the king *would*. It was one thing to welcome a strange peasant girl as a daughter-in-law, especially one who could increase the royal coffers simply by speaking. But to invite along the sister who spewed toads? That was a different matter altogether.

She wouldn't risk her sister's happiness. Which was why, when Rose clutched her close, Gemma speared

Prince Giles with a warning glare. She would find him, her look said, and spew all manner of toads at him if he hurt her sister.

Prince Giles inclined his head. The raised eyebrow told her he understood completely.

Rose whispered a few more seed pearls into Gemma's pockets. And then Prince Giles claimed her hand, helped her into the velvet interior of the carriage, and they were off, Rose blowing kisses, Gemma catching them and returning her own.

Then she was standing in the middle of the road, dust swirling and settling on her skin. The cottage door was closed, shutters drawn tight. There would be no tender goodbye with her mother.

She had nowhere to go. Rose, her constant companion, was no longer part of her life. The ache started deep within her, filling her up rather than hollowing her out. She might burst with the pain. The rattle of seed pearls in her pocket was cold and harsh. Unlike their mother, Gemma took no pleasure in the gift.

If she had nowhere to go, then did it matter which way she went? She pulled in a breath, readying herself, when the croak of someone clearing their throat startled her.

"Excuse me, my lady, but might I have a word?"

CHAPTER 2

GEMMA TURNED. She scanned the road, the woods behind her. She even peered up into the sky.

Nothing.

She shook her head, certain her ears—or perhaps the enchanted forest—were playing a trick on her.

The throat cleared again.

"Down here," it said.

At her feet sat a toad. It was a lean, wiry thing, more legs than squat body. And was it ... wearing a sash? One in scarlet that was trimmed in silver?

"I am Sebastian, High Chamberlain of Her Royal Majesty Queen Francesca." The toad extended itself onto its legs and executed a stately bow.

Gemma cast a quick look left and then right. Seeing no one, and not really caring, she gripped the hem of her skirt and curtsied.

"The queen wishes to speak with you," the toad added.

She touched her fingertips to her collarbone in question.

"Indeed, my lady."

She held up her hands, palms skyward.

"I cannot say why." The toad regarded her with a bulbous-eyed stare. "I don't presume to speak for Her Majesty."

Gemma nodded, and when Sebastian hopped down the side of the road, she followed.

He led her away from the village and into the wild grasses that bordered the marsh. The air was heavy, sweet, and smelled of a perpetual spring. She trudged behind Sebastian, and with each step, the mud sucked at her boots as if it wished to steal them.

The toad turned and pinned her with another yellow-eyed stare.

"Humans have such impractical feet."

Gemma considered her muck-covered boots. He might be a toad, but he had a point.

At last, they reached the other side of the marsh, where, in the shade of a weeping willow, a toad was sitting on an old log. Sebastian drew himself to his full toad height and let out a mighty croak.

"May I present Her Royal Majesty Francesca, Queen of the Toads."

Queen Francesca was round where Sebastian was lean, plump and luscious, and if ever a toad might be comely, then Francesca certainly was. On her head, she wore a crown woven from reeds.

Again, Gemma gripped her skirts and curtsied.

"Oh, she is much too polite," Queen Francesca said, her tone dismissive. "Are you certain this is the one?"

"I am, Your Majesty."

The queen let out a croak of frustration. "That can only mean the old crone has lied once again."

Gemma was still clutching the hem of her skirt, wondering if she had offended the Queen of the Toads, and if so, how. But the queen had her gaze trained on Sebastian.

"It would seem so, Your Majesty." His yellow gaze now surveyed Gemma. "I did not witness the incident at the well, but I detected only sorrow when she bade farewell to her sister."

Francesca let out another croak, one that sounded much like *harrumph*. "I should have suspected as much. Tell me, child, do you feel cursed?"

Did she? She couldn't speak, not unless she wanted to release an onslaught of toads. Her few belongings hung from a sling on her shoulder. She missed her sister desperately. She thought of the words the old crone had flung at her—certainly they were a curse.

And yet, did she *feel* cursed?

Gemma shook her head.

"I thought not." The queen hopped forward. At the edge of the log, she paused and scanned the air. In a flash, her tongue darted out and snagged a fly that had been buzzing by Gemma's ear.

Gemma nodded her thanks. The queen blinked and swallowed.

"For my part," the queen continued, "I do not care

why or how you offended the old crone. She has become unreliable in her dotage."

"Or perhaps it's the magic that makes her so," Sebastian put in. "You've said as much yourself, Your Majesty."

Queen Francesca blinked again, her expression resigned. "Or the magic. But there is little we can do about that." She cleared her throat with a croak and turned back to Gemma. "Now, my dear, I sent Sebastian to fetch you because we require your help. It will be far simpler to show you than to explain. Will you?"

Although the question was more of a command—Francesca was a queen, after all—there was a plaintive note in her words, a worry that ate through the regal veneer. Gemma nodded, adjusted the sling across her shoulder, and followed as the two toads hopped in front of her.

She trudged through the marsh, the two toads in the lead. She splashed through the stream, flung muck from her boots, and became far messier than her two companions.

They arrived, at last, in a copse of slender birches behind the stables of the village inn.

There, two boys were shouting and kicking up dust. At first, Gemma couldn't see because of all the debris in the air—she was so very tired of dust. The boys jeered; they were the sort who teased dogs, tipped cows, and tied noisemakers to cats' tails.

And there, in a dirt patch behind the stables, they currently were collecting, cooking, and dissecting toads. All manner of toads, from tiny ones that might balance on a fingertip to great squat ones that would take two hands to heft. All of them caged or caught.

Gemma let out a yelp, and from her mouth, a gentle toad slipped. She lunged to catch it, but it hopped away, down the hill that would lead it straight to the village boys.

"No!" She mouthed the word to no avail.

"Hush, my dear." Francesca landed on her right shoulder. "Save your voice. We'll need it momentarily."

Sebastian landed on her left shoulder, and Gemma looked from one toad to the other. She pointed to the stable yard and then to her own mouth. Were these her toads?

"Some of those poor souls are Her Majesty's subjects," Sebastian said. "But, yes, others may have been born from your mouth. They emerge confused, and that makes them easy prey."

Easy prey. So, every time Gemma spoke, she condemned yet another toad.

She shook her head, hoping they'd read the despair in that. This was not what she had intended.

"Oh, my dear, don't fret so." The queen patted Gemma's cheek, the touch of webbed hand sticky and a bit clammy. "They emerge confused because *you're* confused."

Gemma turned her head just enough to look the queen in her bulbous, yellow eyes.

"It's the way of the magic, how the gift—or curse, if you prefer to look at it that way—works."

Sebastian caught her attention and nodded toward

her apron. "Didn't your sister cry you a pocketful of seed pearls?"

She touched the pocket and felt the reassuring weight of the pearls beneath her fingertips.

"And the gems she left behind for your mother?" he prompted.

Cold, harsh, cruel things. Certainly, they were perfect in every way, but they would never bring their owner any joy. Gemma nodded.

"You shall always speak in toads," Sebastian continued, "but you control their fate with what's in here." He touched a webbed hand to her head and then leaned down to indicate the spot above her heart.

Below them, a cry went up. The boys raced around the yard, possibly chasing down the toad she just released.

"So, tell me, my dear," the queen said, her voice low and seductive. "Does that"—she pointed toward the stables—"make you angry?"

Again, Gemma nodded.

"Do you feel that anger roiling inside you? Do you feel the strength of it?"

With the queen's words, the anger did boil up, so much so that Gemma thought she might choke on it. She clenched and unclenched her fists. She wanted nothing more than to march down the hill, take each boy by the ear and escort both of them to the village elders or to the lord of the manor or to whomever might inflict the greatest punishment.

But no one cared about a few toads. She turned again to look at the queen. Francesca's eyes were burning.

Whoever had said yellow was the color of cowardice had never locked gazes with the Queen of the Toads.

"Do you want to unleash that strength?" the queen asked.

Gemma gave one emphatic nod.

"All you need is a battle cry."

A battle cry?

"It doesn't need to be words," Sebastian added, "but it does need to be loud."

Loud. She could do loud.

"And ferocious," the queen said. "Think beyond these two ruffians."

Yes. Beyond. She would think of how the forest had stolen her mother, how Prince Giles had stolen Rose, how an old crone in the guise of a fine lady had stolen her words.

She might not have those words, but she could still raise her voice.

"I see that you're ready," the queen said. "Let it out, my dear. Let it all out."

Gemma did. She yelled, the force of it—and the toads —making the back of her throat ache. Her shouts carried beyond the confines of the trees, down the hill, and into the yard.

The boys froze in their task of torturing yet another toad. The creature slipped from their hands and hobbled off, wounded but alive. One boy gaped. The other shook his head, eyes wide with fear, skin sallow as a toad's belly.

It was then that Gemma noticed the toads. This truly was an onslaught. They leaped and hopped, shaking the earth each time they landed. A bullfrog the size of a cat slammed into one boy, knocking him to the ground.

The other boy turned to run, but a contingent of smaller toads landed on his shoulders and his back, their combined strength sending him flying. He crumpled face-down in the dirt, and soon his entire form was covered in writhing green made up of at least one hundred toads.

Gemma scampered down the hill, the queen and Sebastian riding high on her shoulders.

"Oh, well done, my dear! Well done! Look at them, Sebastian. Look at all the wonderful toads!" The queen's voice rang out, her words clear above the cries and the croaking. "Look at my army!"

"Indeed, Your Majesty. I daresay this is a rout."

Careful not to squish a single toad beneath her boots, Gemma marched forward. She yanked the first boy from the ground. With him collared, she proceeded to the next. With a simple wave of her hand, the toads that covered the second boy scampered away. She collared him as well.

"Never again," she said. With each word, a toad sprang from her lips and struck a boy in the face. "You will never harm another toad, cat, dog, or any other crea-ture ever again. Do I make myself clear?"

The first boy nodded so furiously, she thought he might break his neck. The eyes of the second boy rolled back, and he sagged in her grip. She shook him, and he righted himself and joined the first boy in nodding.

"Now, leave!"

With her final words, she let each boy go. They picked

their way across the yard on trembling legs. Once they were clear of the toads, they took off running.

Neither one looked back.

When the dust had settled in their wake, a chorus of croaking filled the air. Gemma stood alone in the yard, surrounded by toads and dust.

Only this time, she didn't mind so much.

CHAPTER 3

HOW LONG SHE STOOD THERE, Gemma couldn't say.
Minutes? An hour? Enough for the sun to creep closer to
the western horizon. Most of the toads hopped off
toward the marsh and the protection—not to mention the
insects—it offered.

Plaintive cries roused her. She looked about. The
queen and Sebastian had left with their army. But here, in
the dry dust of the yard, several toads remained—the
injured, and, yes, the dead as well. Some hobbled to her
and settled in by her feet, almost like a hound might.
Others were too broken to move at all.

Gemma knelt, spread her apron, and gathered the
wounded. The task took three trips, but she transported
all of them to the marsh and found beds for them among
the reeds. Before she curled up beneath the willow tree for
the night, Gemma sprinkled Rose's seed pearls along the
banks of the stream.

In the morning, the sun struck her face as if it had

parted the branches of the willow tree itself. Only it wasn't the sun, but its reflection off an object along the bank, an object that hadn't been there the night before.

It looked like a cathedral or a castle, and it shone in the morning sun, an iridescent white that swirled with pinks and grays. Gemma stared, enthralled. Only after a toad hopped up to the structure and then vanished inside it did she creep closer.

She peered through the opening to discover a tiny hospital. Toads were lounging on beds of reeds. Healthy toads were feeding the injured flies. A few grievously injured ones were struggling to swallow gnats.

"The seed pearls!" Gemma exclaimed.

She couldn't help it. The sight was so wonderful. With her exclamation, two capable toads bounded from her mouth and hopped inside the structure, where they immediately set to work helping the wounded.

She ventured into the village only long enough to buy some bread and cheese. She couldn't stay in the marsh, not for long. It wasn't practical. She wasn't a toad, and a seed pearl hospital wouldn't shelter her. Still, at the moment, it was far better than anywhere else. She stretched along the bank and soaked in the sun without a single fly buzzing her head or a mosquito in her ear.

The toads saw to that.

She sensed the footfalls long before she saw the man they belonged to. The toads grew agitated. She felt the slight tremor of the earth, heard the creak of branches being parted.

She stood and shook the grass from her skirt just as Prince Giles entered the clearing.

He dashed forward, and although Gemma clutched her skirt, there was no time to curtsy. He gripped her by the shoulders.

"It's Rose. They've taken Rose. You've got to help me."

"What?" The word—and the toad—came unbidden. The creature scampered off, scared and alarmed, toward the stream.

"On our return to the palace, we stopped at a village inn for rest and some supper. Believe me, we were cautious, but word about your sister has spread. Bandits waylaid us after we set off again and were clear of the village."

Gemma shut her eyes. Bandits. *Of course.* Rose's gift wouldn't have remained a secret for long. Their mother, for one, would talk. Prince Giles himself had certainly told someone, the King, at least. Speaking of which? She speared him with a look.

Giles shook his head as if reading her thoughts. "My father has ... doubts about Rose's ability. And now that she's..." He trailed off and raised his hands, palms skyward. "I have my own guard but can't dispatch them without his approval."

Gemma crossed her arms over her chest and tapped her foot.

"Even if I could," he continued, "there isn't time. We'll lose their trail if we don't leave now."

"Indeed, you will," croaked a voice. "The Bandit

King moves with the stealth of shadows and the speed of a stallion."

"Oh, you exaggerate," croaked a second voice. "He is but a man, and our girl is clever."

This time, Gemma knew to look down.

At her feet sat Francesca, Queen of the Toads, and her loyal retainer, Sebastian.

Gemma knelt and raised her eyebrows in question. Could these two really help Rose?

"Why, of course we can help you." The queen pressed her webbed hands together in anticipation. "My army yearns to test its mettle against a true foe."

So. Yes. An army of toads. Against bandits. Gemma held back a sigh. Then she thought of the fear in the village boys' eyes. It might just work. She regarded the queen and Sebastian and wondered how they had known she needed help.

"Did you not send us a toad?" the queen asked.

Had she? The one that had leaped from her mouth a moment ago? Well, yes, in that case, Gemma supposed she had.

The queen clapped her hands together, although the sound of it was soft and sticky. "You ride with your sister's swain. We will meet up with you."

"But how—" Giles began.

"You will know the place. We will ensure it." Francesca peered through the woods, her gaze wary. "Besides, I ... dislike horses."

With that, she hopped off, Sebastian following close behind.

Giles turned to Gemma, his expression bemused. "Young swain? I'll have her know that I'm a prince, and my father is king of the realm."

From the woods, Sebastian bounded. He landed with a thump in front of them. "And she is Francesca, Queen of the Toads. Mind yourself, young man."

As if that settled the matter, he hopped off again.

All at once, there was a rustle in the underbrush. The reeds rattled. The weeping willow raised her branches as if in supplication. Gemma peered into the seed pearl hospital only to find it empty, every last toad heeding the call of the queen.

In their wake, the morning went silent except for the persistent buzzing of a single mosquito.

CHAPTER 4

GILES'S WAR mare was fleet, but the road filled with ruts, and Gemma clutched him around the waist as they rode north. They lost the Bandit King's trail at the edge of a deep wood, the mare halting so suddenly that Gemma nearly slid from her perch.

"She doesn't like the forest," Giles said once the dust had settled.

Gemma nodded her agreement. She didn't like it either. The air had a thick, sour taste to it. She thought of her mother, so many years ago, wandering in as one woman and emerging as another.

Her heart thumped hard in her chest.

"Come on, girl." Giles nudged the mare ever so slightly with his thighs. "Let's go."

The horse refused to budge.

"Do you think—?" he began.

Before he could finish, a chorus rose up, croaking and chirping a racket to fill the air.

"My Lady," Sebastian called. "This way. The queen has sent out reconnaissance. They will soon return with news of your sister."

Gemma squinted, scanning the forest for a familiar toad in a royal sash. At last she spotted him in the fork of a dead tree.

"This way," he called again. "And leave the horse. The queen does not wish for her subjects to be trampled."

"I'm not leaving my horse," Giles muttered.

Gemma slid from the beast. Then she tilted her head and skewered Giles with yet another look. She pointed to a clearing, one that was full of lush grass and devoid of even a single toad.

He complied.

They trekked through the woods, Sebastian leaping forward and then doubling back when they couldn't keep up.

"You humans have long and yet such useless legs."

"You may discover, Master Toad, that my feet are less than useless," Giles said. "They can kick a great many things."

"I'm certain they can, sir."

With hands on hips, Gemma turned to face not the toad, but the human behind her. She glared at Giles, wondering if she'd need to start spewing toads at him.

"I can't command my own guard," he said, a hand rubbing his brow, "I can't rescue Rose on my own. But toads? A mere girl? It's humiliating."

Gemma continued to stare and jabbed a finger at her

mouth. Humiliating? Giles, at least, could talk without spewing toads.

The trees shrouded them, and it was too dark to see if Giles blushed or his gaze held any chagrin. He did, however, cough out, "Point taken."

"Excuse me, Your Highness," Sebastian said. "But it's been my experience that it's far better to earn respect than to insist upon it at the tip of a boot."

Giles coughed again, then crouched so he was eye level with Sebastian. "Indeed, Master Toad. I concede your point as well."

Sebastian puffed up his throat in triumph, let out a mighty croak, and continued hopping through the woods.

In fact, a chorus of croaking, calling, and chirping filled the forest, the noise so loud that Gemma couldn't hear her boots crunch the leaves, or her labored breathing, or even Giles who was walking only a few steps behind her.

"Clever of them," he said, voice low. "I'll give them that. If the Bandit King truly is in the area, he won't hear us coming, not with all this racket."

At last, they reached a clearing. At its center, Francesca was holding court, conferring with a small group of toads.

"Come, come!" she called. "My patrol has just returned with news of your sister."

They knelt carefully, she and Giles, checking the ground beneath them for any wayward toads.

"There's a cave to the north," Francesca said. "It's the

Bandit King's main encampment, and that's where he's taken your sister."

"To the north." Giles peered through the trees, his gaze narrowing. "In that rock formation?"

The queen nodded. "Rose appears unharmed."

Giles pushed to his feet. "This should be a simple matter."

"But she's surrounded by at least a dozen men."

He slumped to his knees. "I could fight one man, certainly. Possibly two. Three, depending on their skill." Giles looked at Gemma. "I love your sister. Yes, I know you believe that I love the diamonds more, but that simply isn't true."

She nodded.

He hung his head in defeat. "I can't fight a dozen men."

"Foolish human. Who said you had to?" The queen hopped forward as if to make her point. "The Bandit King will expect to see you, yes? The lovesick prince making a reckless attempt to rescue his betrothed?"

"And?" Giles asked.

"And you'll do just that and be our distraction." The queen gestured to Gemma and then her army of toads. "We will rescue Rose."

He studied Francesca before turning his attention to Gemma. "Do you think it could work?"

She considered the craggy rock formation. In the dark, it loomed over the woods, its shadow menacing. It was just the sort of place a Bandit King might make into a home, so close to the enchanted forest.

But he was expecting humans—and rash ones, at that. He wasn't expecting toads. Really, no one ever expected toads. So Gemma nodded and then shifted so she could curtsy to the queen.

"Ah, excellent. We will strike in the hour before dawn. The men who drink will be well in their cups. Those on guard will be cold and drowsy." The queen let out a mighty croak, and her army responded, once again filling the air with their cries.

Giles returned to his horse to wait for the signal. Gemma rinsed the dust from her face and arms in the nearby stream, then found a spot beneath an old oak. She unslung her bedroll and secured the scabbard with her father's knife about her waist. She sat, arms around her knees, and tipped her head upward, her gaze searching out the stars that peeked through the canopy of leaves.

"Ah, Lady Gemma, may I sit with you?"

Without waiting for a response, Sebastian sprang onto one of the oak's protruding roots and settled in.

"It's a fine thing you do for your sister."

Why wouldn't she rescue Rose? She cocked her head in question.

"I mean to say, to let her go with her prince. He is not worthy of her, not yet, at least. Perhaps one day. Perhaps today will be that day. Who knows?"

Gemma nodded. Yes, who knew? She searched the earth around her for a twig, fingers pushing through the dirt. She found a slender branch and used that to point.

Her aim? The bank of the stream where Queen Francesca was now conferring with half a dozen toads and bullfrogs, all of them meaty in form, their combined brawn obvious even in the dark.

"Her generals," Sebastian said.

Gemma pointed the stick at him.

"Ah, I am not a general," he said, his words filled with regret. "I'm honored to serve the queen in any capacity that I can." He croaked a sigh, and in it, Gemma heard something plaintive and unrequited.

She cleared the ground of leaves and then used the stick to draw a heart.

"Oh! The things you say!" Sebastian hopped from his perch, landed in the center of the heart, and obliterated it with his hind legs. Then he turned a bulbous, yellow-eyed glare on Gemma.

She raised her palms skyward and gave an exaggerated shrug—for, of course, she hadn't said a thing.

Sebastian shook himself. "You know what I mean. I don't love the queen. Well, what I mean is, of course I do, as her loyal subject, and I serve at her pleasure, but—"

Gemma drew a second heart.

"No, no, no! You are a most vexing creature."

"Ah, Sebastian, there you are!"

Both Gemma and Sebastian froze. The queen leaped forward, her intent clear. Before she could land on that outcropping of roots, Gemma swept leaves across the ground, burying the heart she'd carved there.

Sebastian's croak sounded like a whimper.

"It is time," was all the queen said.

THEY CREPT THROUGH THE WOODS, up long and winding paths, until they reached the cave. The toads fanned out so they surrounded the space, toads above, toads below, toads blending in with the rock face at the entrance.

A warm glow spilled from the cave's interior. In the quiet of predawn, Gemma could hear the crackling of the fire, the clatter of boots on stone, the murmur of sleepy conversation.

The sound of pounding hooves jolted her. Giles? So soon? But they hadn't given the signal. Her heart hammered in time with the hoofbeats. Her mouth went dry. Queen Francesca, squatting on her shoulder, murmured, "What has he done? Humans. So impatient."

But the horse that stopped before the cave's entrance wasn't Giles's war mare. Instead, a stallion came to a halt, black as night, and on him sat a man clad in clothes nearly as dark.

"The Bandit King," Sebastian whispered in her other ear.

The man dismounted and slipped inside the cave.

"Well, this is a wrinkle," the queen said. "No matter. Lady Gemma and I will follow the Bandit King. Sebastian, wait for my order, then raise the signal."

"But, Your Majesty—" he began.

"I said, wait."

With reluctance, Sebastian slipped from Gemma's shoulder and hunkered down behind one of the smaller rocks.

"Now, my dear," the queen whispered. "Get us inside."

Gemma inched forward, crouching at first, then on hands and knees. Her skirts tangled about her legs. She grunted, yanked up the hem, and threaded it through her apron.

"You humans have such an odd fondness for coverings," Francesca muttered.

Gemma ignored her.

She crawled along the edge of the cave, where a series of larger rocks shielded her from view. A fire was burning near the center, the flames casting a glow against the cave walls. Shadows were still looming in the corners, but near the fire itself, the circle of light was bright and warm.

She stilled when she caught sight of Rose. Her sister was sitting on a log near the fire, hands bound but mouth free. Gemma soon saw why. At Rose's feet was a pile of gemstones. They sparkled, the diamonds like ice, the rubies like blood.

The Bandit King stood over Rose, a handful of gems in his palm.

"So, gentlemen," he said, and his voice was rich and refined, not at all what Gemma had expected. "Which one of you has harmed our guest?"

A murmur passed through the cave, a shuffling of feet.

"None of us, sir," said a voice from near the back. "Honest."

"Honest?" The Bandit King turned as if he wished to address the entire cave. "Honest?" He was wearing a mask, one with slits for eyes. But Gemma swore his expression was as incredulous as his voice. It was there in the quirk of his lips, the tilt of his chin.

"I expect few things from you, gentlemen, and, yes, ironically, honesty is one of them. Here's my dilemma." He held up a stone between finger and thumb. "Do you see the flaw in this diamond? It's quite visible, even without a glass."

The shuffling grew. Someone coughed.

"And do you know what that means?" The Bandit King turned again, gesturing first at one group, then another. "No one? Ah. What it means, gentlemen, is that our guest was forced to speak under duress."

Oh, Gemma thought. Like the seed pearls that Rose had cried into her pocket and the cold gems spoken to their mother. She shifted, the cave floor sharp against her kneecaps. Her back ached. She cast a glance toward the entrance. What she wouldn't give to move her limbs.

"Not yet, my dear." Francesca patted her cheek. "I'm curious to see what the Bandit King does next."

In truth, so was Gemma.

"I won't ask our gentle guest to identify her tormentor, unless, of course, she desires to." The Bandit King paused and bowed, sweeping an arm toward Rose and letting the gemstones slip from his palm.

Rose was silent, but she glared, first at the Bandit King and then at the assembled group.

"It's just as well," the Bandit King said. "I don't suppose gems spoken in anger would fetch much of a price. So, tell me, gentlemen, which one of you—?"

One loan croak echoed outside the cave, cutting off the Bandit King's words. Gemma patted the spot on her shoulder where the queen had sat. Empty. She scanned the cave floor, the outcropping of rocks, all for a toad with a reed crown on her head. Gemma's heart pounded, and then the ground beneath her did.

Shouts went up. Horses whinnied. Dust swirled, illuminated by both the fire and the early morning light. A moment later, Giles charged into the cave.

"I demand my betrothed! Release her now, in the name of the King and the realm."

The Bandit King swung around, took one look at Giles, and laughed. He pointed a lazy finger toward the prince. "Seize him."

Men leaped to their feet and rushed the cave's entrance. Hunting down Giles was a far better option, Gemma surmised, than facing their own king's wrath.

As quickly as he had entered the cave, Giles fled. The air shook with the pounding of hooves, and more dust filled the space, coated Gemma's face and hair, and fell on the gems like a thin layer of snow. She waited for a beat and then another, making certain all the bandits had left.

She eased from her hiding spot, still on hands and knees. Rose stood, and with quiet steps, tiptoed toward the entrance. Gemma wanted to call after her but swallowed back the words—and no doubt some toads. What if the Bandit King had stationed a guard out front?

She scampered as quickly as she could, all to reach Rose. But when a long shadow fell across her path, Gemma froze.

"Oh, no, you don't." The voice sounded so close that, at first, Gemma thought it was speaking to her.

She hazarded a glance upward in time to see a lone bandit yank a poker from Rose's bound hands. Rose yelped, and a shower of gems clattered against the stone floor.

"You got spirit," the man said. "I'll give you that. But the Bandit King will have my head for those." He toed the gemstones. "Don't even want to pick them up." The man growled a sigh. "And believe me, I never thought I'd say *that* about treasure."

"Humans," a voice croaked in her ear. "They can't shut up."

Gemma cast Sebastian, who had landed on her shoulder, a sidelong glance.

"Present company excluded, of course," he added. "The queen has a plan—"

She never learned what that plan was. The lone bandit stepped away from Rose, his gaze intent on neither her nor the gemstones.

"Hello, what's this? A toad? And an ugly one at that." He reached down and grabbed a plump, comely toad around the waist.

The creature struggled, legs flailing in vain. The man squeezed the toad so hard that Gemma sucked in a breath and held it.

"Love me some frog legs," the man said to Rose. "How about you, missy?"

Gemma's sister doubled her glare. "Stop!"

A single, angry diamond flew from Rose's mouth and struck the man in the chest. He ignored her and merely kicked the diamond across the cave on his way to the fire and the pot that hung above it.

"Oh, my stars!" Sebastian exclaimed. "No. Not the queen!"

Before Gemma could stop him, he sprang from her shoulder, the move taking him across the cave like an arrow. The man stood above the pot, Queen Francesca dangling from his fingertips, her legs beating the air.

The man let go. It was at that moment, when she still hung suspended above the water, that Sebastian collided with her. His momentum sent her flying, her plump body striking the edge of the pot before she landed clear of the fire.

The splash was all Gemma needed to hear. She cried out, and toads burst from her mouth and slammed into the lone bandit while she rushed to the cook pot. Rose regained the poker and, despite her bound wrists, swung it hard into the back of the man's legs.

Unthinkingly, Gemma plunged her hands into the

water. She screamed again, but she caught Sebastian tumbling about in the pot and placed him gently on the ground.

"Oh, Sebastian, Sebastian." Francesca's sobs echoed throughout the cave.

He opened a single eye, its yellow shot through with red. "My Queen. You are ... safe. I ... am ... thankful for that."

"You can't leave me, do you hear me? There's work to do."

"Forgive me, my Queen, but it seems you have one less soldier to command." His words came slowly, laced with both pain and a tenderness that made Gemma's heart ache.

"You ... can't ... leave ... me." The queen's voice shook. "Don't leave, Sebastian. I need you. I..."

He gazed upon his queen one last time and then shut his eye.

"Love ... you." A single sob shook the queen's body, then she pulled herself tall and turned to Gemma.

"Give me an army, girl. Give me a legion of soldiers. I will avenge Sebastian and your sister. They will not soon forget what the Queen of the Toads can do."

Gemma swallowed back her sorrow. Her hands were blazing, the throb pulsing from fingertips to wrist, and she found her anger in that pain. In her mind, she felt the broom strike the backs of her legs, watched the village boys torture the toads, stood by while a prince stole her sister away.

She let her voice fill the cave. The sound came from

the depth of her as if her fury ran from her toes to the top of her head. She cried out until she was spent. The fierce toads that flew from her mouth joined the queen, ready for battle, and they chased the lone bandit from the cave.

He would not be their only target.

Sebastian was still lying on the cave floor. Gemma knelt, and with her hands still throbbing, straightened his royal sash.

"Was he one of your toads?" Rose asked, and with her question came a shower of seed pearls.

Was he? Gemma shook her head. No, Sebastian was —had been—very much his own toad.

Rose gestured to the space around them. "But some of these must be."

A few toads were hopping about, the smaller ones she'd cried out near the end of the queen's command. Gemma shrugged. Perhaps she was their godmother. With toads, who knew?

Hands still throbbing, she pulled her father's knife from the scabbard and hacked away at Rose's bonds. Once free, Rose knelt, spread her apron across the floor, and eased Sebastian onto it.

The plinking of a few more seed pearls against stone caught Gemma's attention. She brushed them—along with a handful of dust—into her palm. The pearls cooled her skin, the fierce red fading to pink, blisters healing almost as quickly as they had formed. Her fingers tingled as if they had been smothered in a soothing balm. She released a sigh and stared at her hands in wonder.

The seed pearls. *Of course.*

"Come," Gemma said, and with her word, a capable toad sprang forth and landed on Rose's apron.

"With him?" Rose glanced down at her apron. "Both of them?"

Ah, even more seed pearls. Gemma grinned for the first time in what felt like days. She nodded and urged her sister from the cave.

CHAPTER 6

GEMMA LED them to the bank of the stream. She sprinkled the seed pearls in a marshy area and set to work
collecting reeds and weaving a bed for Sebastian. The
water lapped at the few angry burns that remained,
cooling them even further.

Rose frowned, confusion marring her brow. Gemma
held up a finger and then urged her sister to turn away, to
concentrate instead on weaving another bed. She was
fairly certain the conjuring of enchanted toad hospitals
was not something one was allowed to witness.

In a moment, it was as if someone had lit a lamp, one
bright enough to chase off the deep shadows of the forest.
A glow encircled them, and when they turned around, a
gleaming structure was sitting on the bank of the stream.

"Oh!" Rose stepped back in surprise, emeralds
pouring from her mouth. "Did we do that?"

Gemma pointed at her sister.

"My pearls, perhaps, and your knowledge."

More emeralds sparkled in the grass, and the toad hopped about, gathering the smaller ones. Once Gemma had placed Sebastian on his reed bed inside the hospital, the toad set about its work. After a moment, it cocked its head at Gemma.

"Do you need some assistance?" she asked.

From her mouth came the answer. Three equally capable toads landed with a plop on the grass. Each gathered some emeralds and bounded into the hospital. Gemma peered in after them, wondering if the emeralds might heal Sebastian—if he wasn't already beyond healing. The toads bustled about, Sebastian remained deathly still, and Gemma tried not to hope too hard.

She looked at Rose and touched her head, her heart, her mouth.

"Yes, I've noticed that too." Rose grimaced as three gems slid from her mouth. "So has the Bandit King."

"Indeed, he has."

That voice, again, so smooth and refined. From the woods, a figure emerged. Backlit by the sunrise, he cut a dashing figure. Gemma had to give him that.

She sprang up, fists tight at her sides, the burns aching ever so slightly. Rose stood middle distance between them. Gemma scanned the forest, the opposite bank. Were they outnumbered, or was it two against one?

She'd take those odds, even against the Bandit King. She reached for her knife.

"Not so fast, Toad Girl," the Bandit King said.

"Don't call my sister that. She—"

In a flurry of movement and spewed amethysts, he

slipped behind Rose, captured her arms, and brandished his own knife.

Gemma froze, held still as if his blade was touching her own throat.

"Now, drop it," he said.

Gemma complied, and her father's knife speared the ground next to her foot.

"That's a good Toad Girl," he said. "Intelligent. Admirable quality, that. I urge you to put that intelligence to use and hear me out."

Rose squirmed in the Bandit King's grip. Gemma narrowed her eyes at him before focusing on Rose. She shook her head just enough that Rose would see. Then she folded her arms over her chest to wait out the Bandit King.

"I do not intend to harm your sister," he said. "Something I'm certain you've figured out."

Gemma jutted her chin at him.

"Ah, you sense my dilemma. Why would I ever release her? Why allow my rivals a chance at such bounty? And truly, it does me no good to have the realm flooded with gems. Rather defeats the purpose of having them in the first place."

Gemma swallowed her despair, the feel of it making her throat tighten. Oh, this was the true curse! Always at the mercy of the greedy and unscrupulous. Always under lock and key. At least as a Toad Girl, she could walk free.

She speared the Bandit King with as fierce a glare as she could muster.

His lips twitched. "Pity there isn't such a demand for

toads." He paused, his gaze flickering over her as if he were considering her full measure. "You convey more with a single glance than most people can with a week's worth of babble. I think I'd enjoy your company immensely."

"You, sir, are a cad!"

Rose's eyes widened. The Bandit King surveyed the woods, mouth tight with panic. Only Gemma knew to glance down.

Sebastian leaped from the roof of the hospital and flung himself at the Bandit King.

For a moment, she thought it might work. For a moment, after Sebastian had knocked the knife from the Bandit King's hand, Rose was free.

Oh, but he was the Bandit King, after all. He snatched Rose around the waist, dashed to his horse, and left them with nothing but a scattering of diamonds, the thundering of hooves, and the point of his dagger stuck in the ground between Gemma's feet, missing her own knife by inches.

"The village!" Sebastian cried. "He must pass through it. Run, my lady. Use your voice. Call out your own army, and have your sister do the same."

Gemma gripped the hem of her skirt and tore through the woods. Every few yards, she halted, gripped a sturdy oak or elm, and cried out, her voice as loud as she could make it. Toads flew from her mouth, their speed and strength like nothing she'd produced before.

They charged ahead of her in leaps and bounds, so that by the time she reached the village, they had the

Bandit King trapped. His stallion was mighty but high-strung. The horse tossed its mane and whinnied in distress while toads pummeled it from all sides.

Gemma cried out again. More toads flew from her mouth—the fiercest ones yet—and headed straight for the Bandit King.

The stallion shied. Rose tumbled from the saddle. After she landed, a battalion of toads flung themselves at the Bandit King, blocking his attempt to grab her. The horse reared, and he gripped the reins with both hands, his face contorted in his effort to control the beast.

Gemma halted in the center of the village, her toads leaping and springing around her as if she were a returning hero. She caught her breath and then yelled.

"Your voice, Rose! Use your voice!"

A knowing look lit Rose's eyes. When the Bandit King circled for a second grab at her, she cried out, her voice clear and sparkling, like the gems that fell from her mouth.

"Citizens of Flane, I bring you great bounty! Behold, the King has graced you with treasure. Come! Fill your pockets! Diamonds, rubies, emeralds, and pearls fit for a queen."

At first, curiosity drew people from their dwellings. But after some children dashed into the road and returned with hands full of gems, every last resident of Flane emerged into the village square.

It was then that Rose made her escape, ducking among the villagers, laughing and speaking with them and offering up handful after handful of jewels. When she reached Gemma, she clutched her tight.

From the opposite end of the village, the Bandit King surveyed them. He had quieted his stallion and now stood next to the beast, a calming hand on its withers. As ever, the mask shrouded his expression, but his mouth was relaxed. Gemma wanted to say he was amused, but she doubted anyone could find humor in the loss of so much treasure.

Then again, maybe the Bandit King could, for he brought his fingertips to his lips and blew her a kiss.

"Until we meet again, Toad Girl." He mounted his stallion. "And trust me, we will."

With that, he rode off, his horse's hooves kicking up dust that lingered in the air long after all the gems and all the toads had vanished from the village square.

CHAPTER 7

"ROSE!"

On horseback, Giles approached, his war mare walking a slow, steady pace. Behind him, bound by the wrist and to each other, shuffled every last one of the bandits—minus their king, of course.

Rose ran to Giles, arms outstretched, her cries of joy producing the finest diamonds the realm had ever seen. The reunion was so tender that the villagers averted their gazes, although they still managed to collect the gems from the road.

When they broke their kiss, Giles plucked a diamond from his mouth.

The villagers cheered.

Giles led the bandits to the Lord Mayor of Flane, and Rose found Gemma.

She stood close and whispered her words. The air was thick with sadness and the sound of seed pearls rattling in Gemma's pockets.

"Come with us, sister." Rose gripped her hands. "I'm certain now that Giles won't mind."

Perhaps not. But what use would she be? What could she do? As much as she longed to stay with her sister, Gemma knew she couldn't go. The palace was no place for a Toad Girl.

"Well, then," Rose continued, although Gemma hadn't said a word. "Promise that you'll at least visit."

Ah, now, that was something she could do. "Of course I will."

With her words, a most comely toad (second only to Queen Francesca) hopped from her mouth and settled on Rose's shoulder.

Rose stared, eyes wide with delight, a finger outstretched to shake the newcomer's hand. "She is like you, sister. Fierce and brave and true."

Gemma shook her head. "Like you," she mouthed and touched her sister's cheek.

She stood by while Giles helped Rose to mount the war mare and swung up behind her. Gemma didn't feel the need to spear him with a glare—not this time. Before he flicked the reins, he brought his fingers to his brow in a salute.

And then she was alone once again, standing in the swirling dust of the road.

"Excuse me, my lady."

Gemma looked down. Then she knelt, and that almost put her on eye level with Sebastian.

"I find that I agree with your sister. You are fierce and brave."

She shook her head and pointed at him.

Gemma was fairly certain toads couldn't blush, so perhaps the hint of pink was the result of his earlier scalding. Still, he blinked once, twice, three times before meeting her gaze again.

She mimicked placing a crown on her head and then spread her hands in question.

"I ... seem to have lost track of the queen, as well as her army."

Gemma scanned the village, the fields, and the woods for any sign of toads.

"It is the way of the magic, I'm afraid. I knew the day might come when I'd lose my connection to her. I find that I'm quite bereft." His gaze flickered toward the road, where dust was still swirling in the wake of Giles's war mare. "We, perhaps, have that in common."

In response, Gemma bent closer and patted her shoulder.

"Are you saying we should journey together?"

She patted her shoulder again.

"I find..." Sebastian croaked. "I find..." He croaked again.

For once, he was a toad without words. And here she was, a girl with only a single toad—at least for the time being.

Sebastian leaped and settled onto her shoulder.

Gemma set off, certain of her journey, if not the path. There were more battles to fight, lovers—she cast a glance at Sebastian—to reunite, and a Bandit King to contend with.

Dust churned and settled behind them. Sebastian's sticky hand came to rest on her cheek.

"That way, I think," he said, pointing west.

His weight on her shoulder, like Rose's seed pearls in her pocket, reassured her. A single toad, this particular toad, was worth more than an entire army of them.

Certainly, he was worth more than all the diamonds in the realm.

A NEW PATH

STRAYING FROM THE PATH

IT WAS A WOLF, rather than an ailing grandmother, that tempted Red into the woods. All day his cries echoed, small, plaintive-sounding things that filled the forest. By the time she found him, night had fallen and the blood on the snow looked black.

By moonlight, she pried his paw from the rusted jaws of the trap. He ran from her. And why wouldn't he? It was her kind that set the trap to begin with. The wolf limped through the underbrush, tail between his legs. Later, if you asked her at what point she fell in love, she would've said that night. At the time, all she knew was how his injured gait made her heart lurch.

Later that night, Red spied his yellow eyes from well beyond the woodpile at the edge of the forest. The next evening, she left a meat pie on the lowest stack of wood. By morning, the tin had been licked clean.

And so went the winter. As the days grew colder and her supplies dwindled, she cut back on her own portion of meat. She could go without, but the wolf was still healing. Now, when she walked in the forest, she never feared brigands or the overly friendly woodcutters. When men called on her, they found the howl of a single male wolf so unnerving that they left their teacups half full, crumb cake uneaten.

When at last the snow melted and the sun heated the earth, Red took to bathing in the stream behind the house. No one dared disturb her. Every night, she set out a meat pie. Every morning, she collected the empty tin.

Except for the morning she didn't. Flies buzzed around the soggy crust, the filling, chewed and pilfered by tiny mouths and claws. She threw on her cape and ventured into the forest—alone.

The trail was easy enough to follow. Drops of blood, tufts of gray fur. The farther into the forest she walked, the slower her steps became. What was done was done. All she could do was delay her own knowledge of it, spend a few more minutes free of a world where, every time she closed her eyes, all she saw was matted fur and severed paws—far too many to count.

That night, for the first time in months, she did not bake a meat pie.

The scratching came when the coals in the fireplace were mere embers. There, at the door, sat her wolf, bloodied but no weaker for his fight. He cocked his head as if to say: *Where's my meat pie?*

She threw her arms around him, buried her face against his neck, and cried until the dirt in his fur became streams of mud.

When the townsfolk came, bearing axes and ropes, she threw open the door for them.

Why, *no*, she hadn't seen any wolves at all lately. In fact, she'd stopped her treks through the forest for fear of them. Instead, she now cared for her grandmother here, in her very own cottage.

The men tiptoed from the room, not wishing to wake the old lady. The women rubbed their chins, hoping old age would not bring such a crop of whiskers.

After that, suitors stopped visiting. Although Red always sent them on their way with a meat pie, they found her grandmother's beady eyes unsettling.

People forgot about Red and her grandmother who, while always ailing, never departed this world for the next. But on moonlit nights, townsfolk stumbling from the tavern swore they heard a woman's laughter mixed in with the howls echoing in the night air.

FIRST PUBLISHED *in Flash Fiction Online and Cicada Magazine.*

GRETEL AND HANSEL

HANSEL WANTED TO GO BACK.

Even after endless weeks in a cage, even after Gretel had scrubbed and swept and scoured for the witch, even after she'd pushed the frog-skinned crone into the oven, Hansel wanted to go back.

They stood at the edge of the forest, where the grass grew wild and sharp, and brambles grabbed at their skin. The trees above reached their branches toward the ground as if they might scoop the two up and carry them away.

"She's dead," Gretel said to him.

Hansel stared into the woods.

"I killed her," she added.

He shook his head, the movement so slow that at first, Gretel didn't take its meaning.

"You didn't kill her," he said, his words as dead as the witch should've been. "She's alive."

Was she? Could she be? Gretel stretched her hands in

97

front of her, palms skyward. These hands. They'd shoved from behind. They'd murdered. The crunch of bones, the sizzle of hair and flesh. The thick smoke that had filled her mouth and throat, the plumes laced with the stench of rancid meat.

No one could live through that. No one except, perhaps, a witch.

"Why do you want to go back?" she asked.

A smile lit his face, the same sort of look she'd seen their father cast toward their stepmother, the same look Millie gathered from men in the tavern, although some of the men reserved that gaze for the pint of ale they held in their grip. When Hansel licked his lips, Gretel hoped he wouldn't answer.

He didn't.

Every year on the anniversary of their escape, Gretel would find Hansel at the edge of the forest. She'd stand with him while the sun dipped below the horizon, the slanting light flickering against the trees, shadows growing and leaping. The branches appeared to elongate as if beckoning them to step inside the woods.

When there was just enough light left to navigate home, Gretel would ask, "Why do you want to go back?"

Hansel never answered.

Every year, she took his hand—a limp, clammy thing —in her own and tugged him from the edge. With each step, her legs ached. With each step, the urge to shove him toward the woods grew stronger.

Go! Run to her!

Only the feel of Hansel's hand in hers kept her steady

on the path home. But maybe she was wrong. Maybe they all were. Hansel lived as if his heart, his soul, still resided deep in the woods, in a gingerbread house. At odd times, she'd catch him licking his lips, and she knew. She'd tasted the sugar too. It had left both of them empty—she without her brother, he without his heart's desire.

The year they turned sixteen, Gretel climbed the path to the woods only to find Hansel's spot empty. Pulse fluttering in her throat, she bent low. Her fingers skimmed the dust trail. In the dim light, she barely made out a boot print. It was enough to go on.

Gretel scampered down the path, grabbed her cloak from the hook inside the cottage door, and raced back up the hill. Before she could catch her breath, before she could gather enough courage to venture into the woods, a hand gripped her wrist.

"Stay back, girl. Don't go after him."

The voice was lilting, filled with sorrow and knowledge. Not her father, then. Gretel turned to confront Millie from the tavern.

"I have to go," Gretel said. "He's my brother."

"Not anymore, he isn't. He hasn't been yours for a very long time." Millie tugged on her wrist, a gentle, coaxing sort of thing that had Gretel stumbling forward. "It's too late. Once the witch has you, she doesn't let go."

"Yes, she does." She wrenched her wrist from Millie's grip and held up her hands for the woman to see. "I did it once. I can do it again."

Gretel pulled her cloak tightly around her and plunged into the forest.

Brambles wielded their thorns like daggers, their sharp points shredding her cloak. Branches grabbed at her hood. Eventually, one plucked it from her head, the force choking her until she undid the drawstring.

On she ran, until the woods opened onto a stream. The stream led to the gingerbread house. Gretel halted, letting the fringe of trees around the clearing conceal her.

The path to the house was covered with brittle, the air perfumed with spun sugar and melted chocolate. Even from this distance, desire churned in Gretel's belly. Yes, she'd tasted the sugar. Yes, she'd thought of returning. But after that unbearable sweetness, the cream curdled in her mouth, the sugar scorched her tongue. She'd purged, not far from here, next to the stream, while Hansel continued to consume the treats as if they were the only thing that could sustain him.

The witch stood in the entryway to her house, but this was not the frog-skinned crone of Gretel's memory. The witch glowed like spring itself, her skin the color of a pale crocus stem, her hair long and flowing, as white as lily of the valley and as soft as spun sugar.

Hansel lounged against the rail, a candied apple in his hands, the fruit so big and bright that it seemed to throw off a glow into the night. The witch curved a finger beneath his chin, and with no more than that, urged him inside.

Gretel threw herself forward, but the rock-sugar fence that surrounded the house barred her way, new segments sprouting across each path she tried. She flung herself against the fence. A second later, she sprang back, her palms stinging. She turned her hands and watched the blood, black in the moonlight, drip between her fingers and onto the ground.

"I've failed him," she said out loud to the forest, for every creature to witness.

"Whoo?" came the soft call of an owl.

"Me. I have. I have failed my brother." Gretel studied her bloodstained hands. Certainly this was proof of that.

"Whoo." The call came again, long and soft, a lullaby rather than an admonishment.

One by one, feathers dropped from the night sky, floating downward until they landed on Gretel's palms. Each feather soaked up its share of blood before disintegrating. When a lone feather landed against her cheek, she sank to the forest floor and fell asleep.

The blaze woke her hours later, the gingerbread house lit with flames. The odor of burnt sugar and charred sweets filled her nose, her mouth, her throat, the stench so caustic, it felt as if a noose had tightened around her neck.

"Hansel?" She called his name again and again, her cries too thin to cut through the thick smoke that billowed from the house. "Hansel?"

Near dawn, the fire burned itself out, the rock-sugar fence now a slag that oozed its way through twigs and leaves. Only the witch's oven remained, squat and low to the ground. It was from there that a figure emerged, its movements as tentative as a newborn calf's.

Gretel leaped across the slag and ran to her brother.

Hansel took her by the shoulders, his fingers thin and

tight. "I had to go back. I had to be the one to kill her." He shook her then as if that would help her understand. "Me, not you."

His blond hair had turned ashen. If she brushed it from his eyes, Gretel thought it might crumble to dust against her fingertips. He reeked of burnt sugar and acrid smoke, but when she turned his palms up, they were clean and pink, like a child's hands.

She took him by one of those hands and led him to the path that would take them home.

First published in Deep Magic, August 2016

HOW GOLDI LOST HER LOCKS

CHAPTER 1

They're going to kill another bear.

That was the only thought in Pippa's head as she navigated the palace's manicured gardens. She ducked behind hedges, avoided the chattering ladies-in-waiting, and held her breath as two royal guards crossed the path in front of her.

Another bear.

The sun beat down, the day already hot, her gown stifling. At least she'd had the foresight to tug on something other than a delicate pair of slippers. The boots? The ones she hadn't worn for months? They felt solid and sure on her feet, and Pippa felt more like herself than she had in ages. She could do things in these boots.

She looked left and right before throwing a cautious glance at the castle behind her. Its shadow followed her as if it somehow knew her plans better than she did. The way clear, she charged ahead, the soft whisper of her gown and the soles of her boots on pebbles the only sounds. At the end of the formal gardens, Pippa shoved her way through a row of hedges and burst through to the other side.

At last she was free of the palace and the shadows it cast. Pippa gathered up the hem of her skirt and ran, escaping into the meadowlands where the tall grasses swallowed her up and red poppies bobbed their heads in recognition.

She made her way parallel to the main road that led into the forest. It was there that the hunting party was loitering. An archer was adjusting a quiver of arrows. Another man was inspecting his sword. They shifted, thick leather boots kicking up dust, their steps imperceptibly taking them away from the trees, a slow retreat that only Pippa could see.

No one had ventured into the woods for nearly a year, not since Prince Bennett had vanished there. The forest had always been enchanted—as Pippa well knew—but now people said that the magic had soured.

The meadow gave way to brush and saplings. She clambered up an incline and took shelter in the shadow of the forest. From here, Pippa reached out a hand and touched the air that held the tang of pine and the warm scent of blackberries. The breeze threaded through her fingers. The magic was ... stronger? Yes. Tinged with something? That, too.

But not sour. Still, it wasn't the same. Something had changed. But Pippa hadn't entered the woods for seven years. A lot could change in that time.

The men continued to waver, dust swirling about their

knees. She crept closer to the smaller, hidden path that led into the woods, her eyes on the men. Eventually, they'd press on. Prince Beauregard had demanded entertainment for the summer fête, and that included a bear for baiting.

Another bear. Like Miven.

She shut her eyes, but that only encouraged the images. Seven years ago, she hadn't been old enough, strong enough, or smart enough to save Miven. At the memory, she touched the scar on her right upper arm and traced its path through the sleeve of her gown. The old wound ached. Was it the proximity of the woods? Or merely her imagination? Perhaps it was her guilt.

She hadn't saved Miven. She hadn't even come close. She thought of the cottage in the woods, homey, clean, and perfect for its occupants. Three of everything. She thought of Old Grizzly, of Brindle, and what had started as a memory of their rough and grumbling growls turned to shouts that echoed across the meadow.

Pippa blinked, drawing her attention back to the hunting party. On the main road, a rider on horseback streaked ahead, two others in his wake. She caught the flash of the royal crest, the red and gold of Prince Beauregard's personal guard. Already the men in the hunting party were taking a knee.

Prince Beauregard's voice rolled through the air on a wave of righteousness and outrage. He spoke at length, the words indistinct although the tone was clear: *Capture a bear or don't bother to return*. Pippa considered her meager plan and the odds she might accomplish it. One girl against a royal hunting party? She glanced toward the men, still on bended knee. This might be the only chance she'd get.

Pippa pushed back the branches and brambles that hid the small path and plunged into the woods.

~

COOL AIR WASHED across her skin. Trees reached for her, branches like spindly arms. Leaves swept across her face and caressed her neck. It was almost as if the forest were hugging her, welcoming her back to the fold.

Seven years. Seven years.

The words were a whisper on the breeze.

Where have you been?

Where had she been? It seemed foolish, now, to have stayed away for so long—despite the injury, her parents' coddling, and even the healer's admonition.

"She shouldn't stray into the forest."

The old woman hadn't elaborated, but then, in Pippa's experience, old women never did. They liked to warn but never explain. Besides, she hadn't strayed in the least. She was marching in deliberately, like a soldier with a plan.

Where have you been? Where have you been?

The little stream took up the chant, babbling it against the polished stones along its bank. The weeping willow joined the chorus, her branches sweeping the earth in a gentle cadence.

"I've been locked away." Pippa kept her voice low in

case the hunting party had entered the woods. "I'm sorry I stayed away so long. I'm sorry…"

Her voice cracked. *Sorry* was such a small and helpless word. It didn't begin to describe how she felt, how the wound in her arm was nothing compared to the one that lingered in her heart.

The stream splashed against the stones. Insects buzzed overhead. The chorus was nearly deafening, but it covered the sound of her footfalls on dried leaves, the twigs snapping beneath her boots.

The forest was opening to her, embracing her. Pippa hiked up her skirt ever higher and raced forward.

She only slowed her steps midway across the log that spanned the stream. The bark was slick. Her boots skidded on its surface, and the log itself rocked. She held her arms out for balance, skirts swirling around her ankles.

"I haven't strayed," she called out, louder now, confident the hunting party wouldn't hear her.

She looked back the way she had come. The forest appeared darker than in her memory, closed off, as if it were rolling itself up behind her. But going back wasn't an option.

"I haven't strayed."

She dashed forward and landed on the other side of the stream before her words faded into the air. Then Pippa grabbed her skirts and ran.

She would not let them take another bear.

CHAPTER 2

WHEN THE COTTAGE came into view, Pippa stepped from the path and walked the perimeter of the yard, keeping well inside the tree line. Seven years was a long time, and the magical curtain that shrouded the cottage from prying eyes had grown thin. That she could see the dwelling so clearly shot fear into her heart.

But then only Miven could weave such an enchantment. That the curtain remained, no matter how threadbare the magic, was a testament to his skill. Even a well-maintained shroud could develop holes. That was how she had discovered the cottage in the first place, all those years ago.

With fingertips, she inspected the curtain. The magic held in places, but if any of the prince's men had an ounce of curiosity, they'd spot the stone path, the tree-stump table set for three, or the latticework and climbing ivy. Then the enchantment would be useless.

Pippa crunched through the underbrush, searching

for a hole she couldn't make worse by slipping through. Some protection was better than none, after all. She found an opening large enough to ease through without resorting to hands and knees. The enchantment shimmered, the vibration like a sigh. Years ago, the tiny tremors in the curtain would have alerted Miven to intruders.

During her first trips through the curtain, she hadn't known that. It was only later, after he had confided that he knew of all her comings and goings, that Pippa had realized that this sort of curtain not only hid but also revealed. And now? Was there anyone left who could read the magic like Miven had?

Pippa entered the yard, and thoughts of intruders, the hunting party, the danger, fled to the back of her mind.

It was almost like coming home. No, it was more than that. It was like returning to the place where you knew you belonged. The air in the yard was quiet and serene. Three tree stumps circled a much larger one, a teapot in its center, around which sat three china cups. On each plate sat a treat wrapped in a soft cloth.

Did they still take tea? Did that mean Old Grizzly and Brindle were alive and well? But three stumps? Three cups? Years ago, there had been—for a while, at least— four, an extra-small one reserved for her. Oh, and the treats! Honeycomb and blackberries, cakes made from oats and brown sugar.

Pippa crept through the yard, barely daring to breathe. Each time she inhaled, the past insisted she pay attention to it. Warm bread and wood smoke, the rich scent of Miven's porridge laced with those sweet blackberries. They would stain her fingers and mouth purple, and Brindle would laugh at her.

Bears, of course, never suffered from such indignities.

On tiptoes, she approached the cottage. She dropped the hem of her skirt so she could cup her hands and peer through one of the windows. Three stools at the kitchen table. Three cozy chairs next to the hearth. The rag rug she herself had knotted.

Three. Why three? The thought had her gripping her skirts and backing away. Miven was dead. She'd seen him die. Pippa retreated to the center of the yard, lifted her chin, and tried to gauge the magic.

Oh, she was out of practice. What had come naturally to an eleven-year-old felt so elusive now.

"I've stayed away too long," she said.

"You certainly have!"

A blur of striped fur barreled into her. Paws gripped her waist and locked around her knees. The creature rumbled and grumbled. No one, Pippa thought—in the instant before she hit the ground—had heard the sound of true happiness unless they had heard a bear laugh.

She tumbled across the yard, skirt tangling with her legs, hair escaping from its coil until she and her assailant bumped against the tree-stump table, gasping and spent.

"You're back!" Brindle hopped to his hind legs. He jumped first onto his stump and then the table, his weight rattling the teapot and cups. "I knew you'd come back!"

Pippa stared up at him. In seven years, he hadn't

changed. Didn't bears grow? Of course they did, but here was Brindle, as big-eyed and round-faced as a cub.

"Old Grizzly!" Brindle cried out. "It's Pippa! Pippa's back!"

On the walkway that led to the cottage, Old Grizzly stood, one giant paw engulfing the head of a cane carved from a thick branch.

"So I see." The old bear looked her up and down. "Our golden-haired girl returns to us. How have you been, my dear?"

Pippa could only nod, for if Brindle hadn't aged, then perhaps Old Grizzly had taken on the task for him. His muzzle was so gray, it appeared nearly white. The cane was much more than the mere affectation of seven years ago. She stood, brushed leaves from her gown and twigs from her hair, and approached.

When she reached him, Old Grizzly enveloped her in a hug. His paws could crush her skull and snap her ribcage like kindling. His claws and fangs were fearsome things. But Pippa never felt more cherished than when she was with Old Grizzly.

"I'm sorry—" she began.

"Hush, child."

"But I never—I mean, I should explain—"

"I understand more than you may realize."

She swallowed hard, pushing both the apology and the explanation back down her throat. Yes, Old Grizzly had a way of knowing things.

"I hear the chatter, the squirrels, the birds. They tell

me things. They've told me how you've grown, how you've healed, and about your life in the palace."

Pippa supposed they could, after a fashion. She preferred life outside the palace, in the gardens or the stables, on the training fields—anywhere, in fact, where the denizens of the court were not.

"I don't like it there," she said, the words coming out with more rancor than she had intended.

"Then, come live with us!" Brindle called. He had busied himself with some honeycomb, and his snout was glistening from his efforts.

"Yes, I should, shouldn't I?" Pippa said brightly, as if Brindle's suggestion was at all practical, as if it didn't pierce her heart.

When he went back to his honey, she took a step closer to Old Grizzly and lowered her voice.

"And Brindle? What is ... I don't understand."

"He is still the cub he ever was."

"And you?"

"I have long since outlived my usefulness."

She opened her mouth to protest, but the old bear continued. "You know it's true, Pippa. Brindle's eyes are clouded, but yours are not. I am old. I'm long past due a permanent hibernation."

She pushed back the well of tears that threatened to flood her eyes. "I still don't understand."

"Do you feel the shift in the magic?"

She nodded. "When did it start? Was it after...?" She couldn't finish the sentence, couldn't say the words *after Miven died*. Not out loud.

"About the time your family took up permanent residence at court."

Pippa tilted her head and gave Old Grizzly a pointed stare.

He raised a paw. "I hear the chatter."

"Or did you send out spies?"

She meant it as a joke, to make him laugh that great, rumbly laugh. But at that moment, she swore he appeared even older.

"You are ... linked to us, in so many ways." He placed a paw on his chest. "For a time, we had a family, didn't we?"

Her throat tightened.

"I cannot influence what happens beyond the forest," he said, his words laced with that low growl she knew so well. "These days, I can barely influence Brindle. But I can keep track of a beloved daughter."

And now the tears did threaten. She would cry, or, more likely, sob. But at that moment, the crackle of underbrush just beyond the yard brought renewed fear and urgency. The hunting party! How could she have forgotten?

"The cottage." Pippa waved her hands as if she could shoo both Old Grizzly and Brindle inside with a single gesture. "A hunting party in the woods, on Prince Beauregard's orders. They're looking for—"

"Yes, child, we know. It's why we cut our walk short."

"But the curtain." Now she flung her hands wide, indicating the enchantment—or the lack of it. Sunlight was streaming through the holes, hot and unrelenting.

Brindle was rolling on his back in one of the spots where it heated the earth, unconcerned and unaware.

"It will suffice. And if it doesn't, the cottage will."

"They'll trap you inside," she insisted.

"Perhaps, but the forest has never been kind to those who intrude." Grizzly raised a paw, gesturing toward one of the dark paths that led to the cottage. "And now? It is not always kind to those who belong."

"But—"

"If Prince Beauregard's party finds us, they won't stay long. We will be fine."

She was about to agree, about to relax, and when Old Grizzly swept a paw toward the tree-stump table, about to take him up on the offer of tea. Before she could, a rustling came from the woods, a crunching and a crashing.

It was a fierce sound, the sound a dozen feet made when trampling underbrush. Pippa spun around, opening her mouth to shout a warning to Brindle.

The long shadow cast across the yard froze her in place. Black and menacing, the form loomed, seeming to melt into the woods that surrounded it. For the second time that day, Pippa forgot about the hunting party.

Standing in front of her was a bear identical to Miven.

CHAPTER 3

MIVEN IS DEAD.

That was her only thought. Miven was dead, and as such, couldn't be standing here, glaring at her with coal-dark eyes. A ghost? One bent on revenge?

Or perhaps everyone was right. The magic had soured, and this was the result.

"Pippa, let me..." Old Grizzly began.

But she was already shaking her head, the buzz in her ears so loud that the sound swallowed the rest of Old Grizzly's words. Miven was dead. She had held him while he died. That had been the worst day of her life.

Until now.

Pippa ran. She leaped over the tree stumps, her skirt rattling the teapot and cups. She plunged through the hole in the curtain and bolted into the woods.

Branches scratched her arms and slapped her face. She welcomed the pain and ran even faster. She longed to outpace the thing dogging her heels, but it wasn't fear that propelled her forward. As malevolent as this faux Miven appeared to be, she didn't fear him. If he wished to tear her limb from limb, she might even welcome it.

No, it was something else that drove her through the woods, something balled tight in the pit of her stomach, where it had festered for seven years. Only now, with the appearance of this other Miven, had it bloomed.

It was something she couldn't outrun.

It was her fault Miven had died.

Each time her mind touched upon the idea, she recoiled, and spurred her legs on faster.

My fault.

She ran until her legs grew weak and her feet unsteady. The toe of her boot caught on a tree root, and her momentum sent her soaring through the air. She landed hard, palms smacking against the earth.

There she stayed, on hands and knees, panting, her breath rough in her ears, her throat parched, limbs trembling. At last her breathing calmed, and the sounds of the forest replaced her panicked gasps—birdsong and the hum of a dragonfly, the scratching of tiny claws against bark.

The steady footfalls of something much larger.

Pippa pushed to her knees and hazarded a look over her shoulder. There, shrouded by leaves, was a silhouette, one the size and shape of a black bear.

One that was headed straight for her.

The bear's pace was slow, deliberate, as if he knew he had all the time in creation, as if she was his only concern.

Perhaps he'd been waiting for this day, for a time when chance or fate or the soured magic would return her to these woods.

Pippa pushed to her feet. Her knees buckled, but she embraced a stout oak and stopped her fall.

She pulled in a breath, tested the ground beneath her boots, and ran again.

The moment she veered left, Pippa knew it was a mistake. A felled tree, one wider than she was tall, blocked the path. She glanced left, then right, but the best way—the fastest way—was up and over. She lunged, rough bark scraping her already sore palms, splinters stabbing beneath her fingernails.

She scrambled to the top and froze.

Brambles wove across the space below. How deep was it? Pippa peered through the tangle of thorns and leaves, searching for a hint of ground. Did the path continue, or was this the end of it?

Behind her, the forest trembled in the wake of the bear. His footfalls continued at that rhythmic, deliberate pace, as if he knew the woods had colluded to stop her trek.

Could she jump, then? Would the thorns slice her to ribbons before her toes touched ground? *Would* her toes touch ground? And if so, would the landing shatter her bones?

Still the bear lumbered forward. Branches whipped against each other, zinging, cracking, popping. The scent of fresh green wood reached her. His destruction smelled sweet.

Pippa didn't dare glance behind her. She'd need her wits and all her focus if she were to jump. If she saw Miven, saw his face, grief might weaken her legs and sorrow would steal her breath.

She inched forward on the log. The grooves in the bark were deep enough to catch her feet, like so many hands grabbing. She sent up a small prayer of gratitude that she had thought to wear the boots today and then jumped.

She had forgotten about her hair.

Pippa plummeted, the strands fanning out behind her. She covered her eyes, fingers tight against the lids, but the thorns weren't interested in blinding her. Instead, they latched onto her hair, catching the strands like a fine-toothed comb, grasping and tugging.

Pippa felt the sting against her scalp before her boots met the earth below. When her toes did touch down, she found herself balancing on their very tips.

Around her, the locks of her hair were spread, a canopy of burnished gold. She took quick, shallow breaths. Anything deeper, and the sting returned, the sharpness racing along her scalp. She held still, heart thudding. Even that, even the coursing of her blood, was too much.

She no longer heard the footfalls behind her. The bear had not followed her path. He knew these woods and must have known that the way through was not up and over.

The bear was winding his way through the dense

greenery, avoiding the log altogether. Yes, he knew this forest, and it knew him. She'd stayed away far too long.

Seven years. Seven years. Where have you been?

The bear that looked so much like Miven paused as if he heard the question in the breeze. He approached, lumbering from all fours to standing upright on his hind legs.

Then he halted in front of her, close enough that she caught his scent—warm and musky and sweet, like standing in the very center of a blackberry patch on a hot summer day.

She couldn't read anything in those coal-dark eyes. And while he hadn't lost the fierce look of a predator—Miven had always appeared fierce—his lip was uncurled. No snarl issued from his mouth.

He simply stood before her and waited.

CHAPTER 4

TEN YEARS EARLIER ...

When had it all started? When Pippa discovered she could wander the fields behind the village unattended? When her parents had become so consumed with their duties at court that they paid no heed to a middle daughter whose only distinguishing quality was hair the color of sunshine?

Or was it when the woods first beckoned?

She'd been cautious at first, keeping the village well in sight, skipping a few feet inside the forest and scampering back out. But every time she did, the willows would sweep the earth, the sound like laughter. Squirrels chattered at her, tossed acorns for her to catch. Everything about the woods welcomed her.

So one day she stepped inside and kept walking.

The forest brought her to clear streams when she was thirsty, fed her raspberries and blackberries when her stomach rumbled. And when she had exhausted the company of rodents and birds, it brought her to a cozy cottage shrouded in an enchanted curtain.

Pippa hadn't dared touch a thing. She stood first in the yard and then inside the cottage itself. (In her defense, the door *had* been unlocked). She soaked in the feel of the place. The air was serene, and at the same time, rich, like it held the aftereffects of Old Grizzly's stories, Miven's honey cakes, and Brindle's laughter.

The three bears found her like that, standing in their kitchen, hands clasped beneath her chin as if she were making a wish.

In truth, she was. She wanted to meet the occupants of this little cottage.

The woods obliged.

The bears hadn't growled or even scolded, but simply stared at her, Old Grizzly with a squint, Brindle in amazement, and Miven with a knowing look.

"It seems, gentlemen," he said, low and grumbly, "that we have a guest." Then Miven had bowed in welcome as if she were a queen.

For three years, Pippa returned, daily when she could. For three years, her heart was so full of wonder and love, it felt like it might burst from her chest.

She took lessons with Brindle and became so adept at doing sums and calculations in her head, she outpaced all the boys in the village school. Miven set new tasks for her, taught her how to navigate the forest, how to read its moods. She sat at Old Grizzly's feet and soaked in his stories of old. She played so rough and tumble with Brindle that she became fleet, crafty, and strong. The only things she lacked, in her opinion, were fur and claws.

And then, a hunting party caught Brindle. Pippa had stumbled upon them by accident—or perhaps the woods had led her to them. She heard his cries first. Even after the men managed to muzzle him, his sobs filled the forest.

But an eleven-year-old girl against a party of grown men? No matter how fleet she was? It was no match. Brindle's eyes beseeched her as she crept through the underbrush. She tried to tell him: she'd go get help; she'd go get Miven. Miven, of course, could fix anything.

She scampered off toward the cottage and found him in the kitchen, the air redolent with warm bread and fresh honey.

"They have Brindle."

It was all she had to say. He knew, as Miven always did. Brindle had wandered off, or—more likely—had been lured by some sweet treat. Miven burst through the kitchen doors, racing forward on all four paws, his claws churning up the earth.

Pippa ran after him, heart pounding from exertion and fear, her legs barely able to keep up with the galloping bear.

What happened next, she was never quite sure. Two bears, one girl, six men—and fur and ropes and a cruel-looking muzzle. Miven had thrust Brindle at her; that, she remembered. The weight of him sent her staggering backward, but somehow she had remained on both feet.

She held the baby bear tight, fingers working to undo the muzzle, his cries sharp in her ears.

She sent Brindle into the woods with a shove. He knew enough, was scared enough, to run straight for the cottage. Then she turned, ready to confront the men, to raise her chin and place a hand on her hip—the way she'd seen the Queen Mother do—and scold.

But Miven was standing on his hind legs, his front paws bound tightly with a length of rope, a muzzle shoved over his nose and mouth.

A noose around his neck.

Pippa shouted, but it was as if the men didn't hear her. They joked and jeered, their laughter reaching the canopy of trees, where it seemed to fester. Squirrels pelted them with pebbles. Crows dipped and dived. The men walked on, except for one who shooed her away so she stumbled from the path and landed in a thicket of brambles.

Her ankle twisted beneath her, the pain adding to the chorus around her. She limped and ran after the men, emerging from the forest into a cluster of rowdy children and curious villagers. The hunting party continued across the bridge and into the village square, and the crowd grew around them.

Someone had dogs at the ready, the hounds straining at their leashes. They snarled and growled and snapped at the air. The tavern keeper sent his barmaids into the square, their fists gripping steins of beer. Another man was taking bets on how many dogs it would take to slay the bear.

Pippa shoved her way through the throng. Someone stepped on her foot. Someone else sent an elbow into her stomach. A rush of quicksilver washed across her tongue. When she went to wipe her mouth with the back of her hand, she left a smear of red across her skin.

She reached the front, where only the men and older boys were standing, her only thought to save Miven.

Later, Pippa would review those moments, look at them from each angle, chastise herself for what she had missed, how stupid she had been. For had she been smart, she would've created a distraction, uncorked the kegs in the tavern. Had she been clever, she would've crept into the butcher and pilfered a slab of pork to tempt the hounds away. Had she been cunning, she would've set any number of merchant stalls on fire.

She'd been none of those things. She'd only been a girl whose heart was too full and too heavy with sorrow to do anything but throw herself at the object of her affection.

She raced into the square and locked her arms around Miven's neck. Her fingers were far too puny to loosen the noose that choked him, but she tried, the rope rubbing the pads of her fingertips bloody.

A cry went up behind her. Shouts echoed against cobblestones. People scrambled, but no one approached. Pippa hadn't thought what might happen until the first arrow hit Miven in the side.

His body shuddered with the onslaught. One arrow after another. Miven shook his head as if he meant to dislodge her. Pippa refused to let go.

"Fools!" someone called out. "You'll hit her!"

Still the arrows came.

Until, at last, one pierced her arm and lodged in Miven's chest. It was the spot, Pippa knew, above his heart. The bear stumbled, sank to one knee, and then fell onto his back. She went with him, the arrow locking them together in a deadly embrace.

Miven's blood ran thick and hot, and Pippa swore it smelled not of copper but of blackberries. Her cheeks stung from tears, from Miven's fur as she buried her face against him.

She knew the minute her blood touched his. The world shimmered. The noise faded, and it was as if the two of them were alone in the woods, resting after a long walk.

My blood will protect you.

The words came with one final sigh. And then Miven was gone.

No one ever mentioned that day. Pippa was never punished for straying into the woods. Perhaps her parents thought a two-month convalescence was punishment enough. But the event in the village square followed her. That, she knew. Chatter cut short when she entered a room. Whispered words flowed behind her back: *bear* and *forest* and *scar*. Neither time nor concoctions helped. The skin the arrow had pierced was as jagged and puckered and angry as ever.

And if, after everything, she made fewer friends at court because of gossip and scars, Pippa didn't mind.

And now? Seven years later? With Miven standing in front of her? She wanted to shake her head, shake away the images of all those years ago. The brambles tangled with her hair, gripping it ever harder. The pressure built in her scalp. Tears escaped her eyes and traveled down her cheeks.

"I didn't mean for it to happen like that," she said. "I only wanted to save you."

Miven tilted his head as if he was examining her.

"If I could change things, I would. I would have the arrow pierce my heart instead of yours. I shouldn't say this, except that it's true. I loved ... love you most of all."

First one tear and then another traveled down her face. Already, the skin on her cheeks was raw. She held still, let the tears roll unimpeded, let the thorns pluck strands of hair from her scalp. None of this could hurt half as much as the dozen arrows that had felled Miven.

Still on hind legs, he padded closer, his footfalls soft against dead leaves. He snuffled as if breathing her in, remembering her. Then he raised a forepaw and brought it to her cheek.

Pippa's pulse beat hard in her throat. She blinked away the tears, tried to gauge his intentions. Miven brought his paw closer, and, yes, there was that blackberry scent she knew so well. For a second, she closed her eyes, and seven years faded away.

When his fur grazed her skin and soaked up a tear, her eyes flew open. Around them, the world shimmered, like it had when Miven's blood had touched hers. His form faded, the fur becoming translucent, the image of him like stardust.

In his place, surrounded by that stardust, stood Prince Bennett.

CHAPTER 5

FOR A MOMENT, all Pippa could do was gape. Prince Bennett, heir to the throne, lost and presumed dead, for certainly no one had come forward demanding a ransom for his return. He was here, in the enchanted woods.

Then she remembered herself.

"Your Highness." The words came out in a croak. Her skirt was hanging in tatters around her, but she gathered it as best she could. She was half-committed to a full curtsy when a flash of pain raced across her scalp.

Prince Bennett held up a hand. "Under the circumstances." His gaze took in the halo of her hair, then traveled downward to where his leather boots transformed into black bear paws. "Yours and mine. We'll ... dispense with formalities."

"But ...?" Now that the pain had subsided, one mortifying thought took its place. She'd just told the crown prince that she loved him! No, that wasn't true. She had been speaking to Miven, or a creature that looked like Miven, or Miven's ghost.

Oh, she was so confused. "I don't understand ... and I thought you were—"

"Someone else entirely." His mouth curved in the barest hint of a smile. "That was quite clear."

"Do Old Grizzly and Brindle know? I mean, do they think you're a bear?" Pippa peered at him through the haze of stardust. And, yes, the telltale signs betrayed themselves, especially around the eyes. Prince Bennett's were as coal-dark as Miven's, but they gazed upon the world in a much different manner. There was no contentment in the prince's gaze the way there had been in Miven's.

"Old Grizzly's far too clever not to know." The prince paused, considered for a moment. "And Brindle is too innocent. If he suspects, it's not a thought he wishes to entertain. He is only happy that Miven has returned."

"So, are you Miven?" Pippa studied him and the outline of the bear that seemed to wax and wane. "Your Highness," she added hastily.

"For all intents and purposes, I suppose I am."

Perhaps it was his smile, both self-deprecating and self-assured. Perhaps it was the fact she'd always preferred Bennett to Beauregard; that it was, as her father said, the difference between a strong hand and an aggressive one.

Prince Bennett, alive! That was something. He could return to the kingdom and rule once the old king had finally breathed his last. Things would be right again. She might even enjoy her time at court. The notion reassured her.

Until she remembered the hunting party.

"Sire, there's a hunting party. You must..." She looked about—or tried to—and the brambles gripped her hair tighter. She cried out and then sighed.

"I know," he said, with what sounded like both resignation and regret.

Pippa opened her mouth to speak, then shut it. Her mind whirled. She pulled the pieces of the puzzle together, and what she constructed made her skin break out in gooseflesh; icy dread filled her stomach.

"You were also on a hunting party when you vanished, were you not?"

"I was."

"And now your brother has sent yet another party, one to procure a bear for the summer fête."

"He has."

"Does he intend—?"

Prince Bennett held up a finger. "Treason is punishable by death." The finger transformed into a claw and then back again.

Pippa clamped her mouth shut.

"It's a pity I can't prove he committed it."

She drew in a quiet breath and considered his confession. "Then?"

"I am stuck in these woods."

She stared upward at the golden canopy that surrounded them. A sparrow had landed on a far-up branch and was pecking at a few strands of hair as if it wished to whisk them away for its nest.

"As am I," she said at last.

Chagrin flashed in his eyes. "Oh, Lady Pippa, forgive me. You've been tethered here the entire time we've been speaking."

"And the hunting party is still in the woods."

"I suppose they are, but they don't concern me now." Prince Bennett surveyed the brambles and thorns and the strands of hair that seemed to reach all the way to the sky.

While he studied her, Pippa ventured, "You know ... who I am?"

"Your father is ... was on my privy council. As for yourself? Pippa Lane, with hair of gold, skin of honey, mind as sharp as a dagger? You're not without your own reputation at court."

The flush started at her neck, flooded her cheeks, and burned across her forehead. If Prince Bennett noticed, he didn't say. Instead, he circled her. He reached first one hand and then another into the tangle of thorns and strands.

Each time he did, fingers became claws, and a deft hand transformed into a clumsy paw.

"And now it seems I can't even free a damsel in distress."

He stepped back, a frown furrowing his brow, and the resemblance to Miven was so striking that her breath caught, and her heart thumped in recognition.

And yet, he was still the prince. He was still wearing

136

leather boots and had his sword strapped to his waist. He had ventured into the woods all those months ago presumably to hunt. If a man like Prince Bennett ventured anywhere, he went prepared.

"Sire, do you have a knife?"

CHAPTER 6

PRINCE BENNETT REMAINED silent for so long, Pippa wondered if he had heard her.

At last, he leaned down and withdrew a dagger from a sheath hidden by his boot. He held it up so sunlight glinted off the blade.

"You mean like this?"

"Exactly."

"I don't think—" He glanced down at the dagger in his grip and shook his head. "I can't predict the transformations. I may end up cutting you—or worse."

Pippa held out her hand. "I'll do it."

He considered the tree that had her tethered, his gaze roving from branch to branch, back and forth, and finally centering on her face. "Perhaps you should."

They were only standing a few feet apart, close enough that the air still held a hint of blackberry. This was a simple exchange. Even so, when Bennett passed her the knife, the hilt slipped from what looked like claws and dropped straight through her fingers.

She leaped back, her scalp on fire with pain, and watched as the knife landed between her feet, blade stuck in the earth.

Prince Bennett swore. He bent to retrieve the knife only to have his paws swipe and grabble without grasping it.

"Please, sire," Pippa said. "I'll get it."

He stared up at her, one eyebrow raised. "Will you, now?"

She made it halfway before her hair stopped her.

They stayed like that, Prince Bennett on one knee before her, Pippa hanging by her hair, fingers skimming the air above the hilt of the dagger.

Then he started to shake, his laughter rich, warm, and infectious. She felt the giggle well in her throat. She wasn't that sort of girl, tittering whenever a knight—or prince—glanced her way. But under the circumstances?

She laughed.

"We are rather ridiculous, aren't we?" he said.

"I'm afraid so, Your Highness."

He looked on the verge of saying something more when the crunch of the underbrush froze them both.

Prince Bennett put a finger to his lips. She nodded—as much as her hair allowed—to show she understood.

Instead of standing, he dropped to all fours. The transformation was nearly instantaneous. One moment, he was the prince, traversing the woods on hands and knees. The next, Miven was barreling through the undergrowth and emerging on the other side with a deafening roar.

A high-pitched yelp echoed, followed by the sound of scrambling feet, the crack of twigs and branches.

Upon his return, Miven faded into Prince Bennett once again, the ever-present stardust sparking around him. Pippa stood open-mouthed at how quickly and completely man changed into beast and vice-versa.

"One of Beauregard's men. He'll return with the rest of the party," he said. "It's possible he saw us both."

"Then, you should return to the cottage, sire. You have time, and I'm certainly enough of a distraction."

His mouth formed a hard line. "Yes, that's what I'm worried about."

"They'll have to free me before chasing after you. I don't understand—"

"I'm not leaving you here with Beauregard's men in the forest." He delivered this with all the authority of a king and all the fierceness of Miven.

Pippa raised her chin. "And I'm not letting them kill you again."

She knew it was nonsense even as the protest left her mouth. Prince Bennett wasn't Miven. And yet, there was a reason he appeared to be so. Which meant that maybe there was a reason she was here in the woods, today of all days.

Perhaps he felt it too, for he nodded in what looked like a concession. Or as much of one as a prince was capable of.

They both stared at the knife.

He swore again and said, "Think fast, Lady Pippa."

With the toe of his boot, he launched the dagger into the air. It spun once, twice. The blade sliced through the stardust and left it glittering in its wake.

How she caught the hilt and not the sharp edge, Pippa couldn't say. How she caught the knife at all was a mystery. It felt solid and sure in her palm. When she brought the blade to the first strands of hair, it sliced them like a scythe through wheat.

Lock by lock, she severed the bonds that had held her in place. Lock by lock, she rid herself of what her mother referred to as Pippa's "one true beauty" and the key to making an advantageous match. After she sliced through the final lock, she tossed the knife into the air just to watch it spin again and caught it deftly a second time.

Her head felt so light. She rubbed a hand over her scalp as she returned the knife to Prince Bennett. She marveled at the feel of the short strands beneath her palm.

Oh, certainly there would be consequences once she returned to the palace. Her mother, for one, would be beside herself. Pippa could taste the recriminations already. Even so, it might buy her what? Another year, possibly two, when she wouldn't have to fend off suitors? A wave of giddiness filled her. No one—at least no one in Prince Beauregard's court—wanted a girl without any hair.

A fluttering above her head caught her attention. She and the prince both looked up in time to see that industrious sparrow, along with several others, pluck the strands of her hair from the brambles and spirit them away.

"No time to mourn the loss now," he said.

"Trust me, sire. I'm not."

He regarded her, lips pursed as if holding back a smile. "No, I don't suppose you are." Then he extended a hand. "We must venture farther into the woods. That's our only option for now."

"Will they follow us?"

"I hope not."

She took that proffered hand, and its grip was solid and sure and so very warm. But before they could clear the thicket of brambles, something whizzed past Pippa's head.

An arrow lodged itself in an oak mere feet away, its thud sending fear into her heart. She glanced at the prince, and the stardust before her eyes wavered. For an instant, she saw Miven, felt the impact of a dozen arrows, watched his blood stain cobblestones.

A second arrow flew past, this one catching on the sleeve of Pippa's gown, slicing the material and scratching her skin.

The pain cleared her head, and she swallowed her yelp of surprise. A thin line of blood bubbled to the surface of her skin, and the sting radiated along her arm.

"Damn," Prince Bennett muttered. "I think they mean to surround us."

They crouched low, and the next volley of arrows soared over their heads.

"What do they see?" she asked, her voice no louder than a whisper. "A man or a bear?"

"A bear, would be my guess."

"Then, why wouldn't they cry out, attempt to save me from you?"

"I don't know, but it does not bode well."

No, it didn't. Neither did the creeping footfalls that, as Prince Bennett had predicted, surrounded them. Blood trickled down her arm. She moved to wipe it away, but her hand froze above the wound.

One, two, and then three drops fell to the earth. Only then did her hand move. Only then did she catch the blood with what remained of her sleeve. Something shifted in the undergrowth, something lush and green and full of life.

The earth rumbled beneath them, and then what looked like a wall emerged from the soil, one of vines and brambles. It moved outward and away, corralling the hunting party, blocking their view, blocking their path, blocking their deadly arrows.

"Gods and stars," Prince Bennett muttered.

"What is it?" She blinked in disbelief, but the vines continued their onslaught.

He exhaled in what sounded like an equal mix of amazement and admiration. "Our way out."

He tightened his grip on Pippa's hand. "I know can run, Lady Pippa, but the question remains, will you follow me?"

With her free hand, she hitched up her skirt. Again,

she sent up a silent prayer of thanks for the boots on her feet.

"Yes," she said. "I will follow."

T HEY RAN, only stopping to scoop water whenever they crossed the little stream. It babbled at them, or at least, it seemed to.

Welcome back! Welcome back! Run faster! Hurry!

They plunged ever deeper into the forest, doubling back on themselves, pausing for the briefest moments so Prince Bennett could tilt his head and listen intently.

"Do you hear like a bear or like a man?" she asked once they'd taken up the run again, words coming between breaths.

"A bit of both. If I'm quiet, I can use the senses of a bear. It's quite remarkable."

"But?" she ventured.

Once again, the stream appeared before them. He slowed their steps so they might drink. He knelt on the bank, hand cupping water, and regarded her.

"I said it was quite remarkable." His tone suggested he wasn't about to elaborate. Pippa ignored it.

"It wasn't what you said, but how."

He sat back on his heels. "Ah, yes, I suppose you're right."

She continued to stare at him, because that wasn't an answer.

"Yes, well, my fear is this. If I'm too quiet, if I slip into the bear's senses too fully, I will leave behind the man."

"Would that be so bad?"

"You tell me, Lady Pippa. How are you enjoying life at court these days?"

The flush assaulted her cheeks, and although they'd been running and she was pink-cheeked already, certainly he noticed.

"The only reason things are tolerable, at the castle and in the land, is because my father still lives. I cannot let the kingdom pass to Beauregard, and no one will crown a bear as king."

She'd prefer a bear as king; they had more sense than most men. But, yes, in the evenings, she heard the worried voices of her parents, hushed words and unfinished sentences. *What if...? And then...? Will our girls...?*

She couldn't even blame her mother—too much—for wanting her to make an advantageous match, perhaps in some other kingdom. But the old king still lived, which meant the center would hold—for now.

Pippa considered the prince and the bear-shaped halo of stardust that surrounded him. "How did this enchantment come to be?"

"I'm not sure that matters."

"Doesn't it? If we know how a thing is made, we can unmake it. Can't we?"

"*We*, Lady Pippa?"

"Yes, *we*, Your Highness."

She was about to elaborate when he held up a hand. His gaze darted first behind her, and then it swept the perimeter. Pippa held her breath, shut her eyes, and searched the forest for any signs they'd been followed.

"Anything?" he murmured a moment later.

All she could hear was the pounding of her own heart, a songbird in the tree above their heads, and the soft, splashing lullaby of the stream.

She shook her head. "You?"

"No, but I don't find that reassuring." He scanned the sky. "It grows dark. We should find a place to rest. I have nothing to feed you, but we could perhaps forage for some berries."

"You don't need to feed me, sire. Besides, that's—"

"Something Miven would do." He pursed his lips as if, once again, he was trying not to smile. "And yet, the urge is undeniable. Come." He held out his hand, and when she took it, he added, "Let's find you some supper."

THEY SETTLED near where the stream flowed into a deep pool. Pippa knelt on its banks and rinsed the grime and blood from her hands and arms, splashed her face with the cool, sweet water, and ran damp fingers through her newly shorn curls.

By the time she finished, Prince Bennett had swept clean a small alcove in the shadow of a boulder. Pine trees stood sentry around the clearing, and a pile of blackberries rested in a basin created by a grape leaf larger than both her hands put together.

"Your Highness, thank you." And because now she was clean—if not entirely presentable—and because they no longer needed to run, and she was no longer tethered by her hair, Pippa executed a deep curtsy.

He regarded the gesture with one eyebrow raised. "I thought we agreed not to stand on ceremony."

She surveyed their camp, and if he wasn't going to smile, well, she could. She raised her gaze to meet his and beamed at him. "Under the circumstances, I don't think it's possible."

"Indeed. Sit." He gestured to the swept earth. "Eat—but not too fast, or you'll get sick."

"That's Miven talking, begging your pardon, sire."

"Is it?"

Pippa plucked a berry from the pile. "As a child, I may have gorged on blackberries, much to my chagrin."

"I may have as well. Of course, now..." He let his words trail off, his eyes focused on the darkening woods beyond.

"As a bear?" she prompted.

"I ate my fill. It is, perhaps, one small advantage to this enchantment."

"Will you tell me? I do want to help you. I know these woods. I knew ... Miven."

He studied her again, his expression thoughtful. "I

feel as if I've intruded into something quite personal. I am not Miven. And yet, both Old Grizzly and Brindle speak to me as if I am, as if I share the same memories of you that they do. They have a great love for you."

"I was a child."

"But have you forgotten?"

No. She hadn't. Of course she hadn't.

"And you love them still," he prompted.

It wasn't a question. Because of course she did. She loved all three of her bears, and each time that stardust halo shimmered around the prince, her heart turned over on itself.

"I daresay it's why you're in these woods with me now. Am I right?"

She gave him a single nod.

"After I first transformed and found my way to the cottage, Old Grizzly spent hours trying to draw out what I knew of you, of your life at court." He tilted his head in further contemplation. "He was unimpressed with my lack of knowledge."

Yes, as if the crown prince had nothing better to do than keep track of a minor nobleman's daughter.

"He said that the squirrels and birds helped him."

"Have you ever chatted with a squirrel, Lady Pippa? No? It's less than enlightening. For instance, we know what it is you enjoy eating, although the squirrels do feel that you could share a bit more of your bounty." He paused, and again, that almost-smile lit his face. "And we know you walk a great deal in the gardens. The birds tell us that."

Pippa laughed. "I will share from now on, and, yes, I enjoy the gardens."

"Alone," Prince Bennett added. "You are often alone."

All at once, her laughter faded.

"So, you see, none of that truly tells them how you are."

Her throat felt tight, and she managed no more than a nod. For a moment, she thought the conversation might end, or worse, she might have to explain herself, but her mind latched onto something the prince had said.

"Sire, when you first transformed? What happened? Do you remember?"

"I remember, but I don't know how significant my memories are. It was a hunting party, although our aim wasn't to hunt, per se, but rather to indulge in some camaraderie. Beauregard said it would be good for me to get away from the demands of the kingdom."

With the king so ill, he had been ruling in his father's stead, and Prince Bennett was perhaps five years older than she was. The weight of the kingdom was a lot for a man so young to endure.

"I agreed," he added. "Foolishly, it seems now. I've never been ... close to my brother. Our interests and temperaments are too different." He settled in against the curve of the boulder, leaned his head back, and stared up at the sky. "And, yes, he has always been ambitious, but I never thought..."

Pippa let him contemplate the stars while her mind

whirled. It was almost as if she could see the two brothers in the woods. "Was it a small party, say six or eight men?"

"It was."

"And did you and your brother stray into the woods alone?"

His gaze returned to her. "Indeed. On his suggestion." He leaned forward. "What is it you see, Lady Pippa?"

She shook her head. "Nothing, and yet—it's like a whisper, a hint of a word. It's there, and at the same time, not." She reached out a hand and touched the stardust that surrounded him. "Like this."

With that touch, she saw completely. Prince Beauregard urging Bennett away from the campfire where he'd been resting quite contently, boot-clad feet on an old stump. Then came a glimmer that rained from the canopy of leaves above their heads. The glint of a knife's blade across a bare palm.

"He swore some sort of oath," she said. "With blood, but to whom or what—" Pippa sighed and shook her head in frustration. "I can't see."

"You saw more than I did. I only remember being caught in what felt like a web. I remember Beauregard bidding me farewell. I remember being lost and confused until I stumbled upon the cottage and Old Grizzly took me in hand." Despite everything, his lips quirked in an almost-smile. "Or paw, as the case may be."

"Why send a hunting party after you now?" she asked.

"Who's to say he did? He may only have wanted to

catch young Brindle for some cruel sport and nothing more."

Pippa considered the few remaining berries resting on the leaf. Her stomach ached, but it wasn't from anything she had eaten.

"You doubt my words, Lady Pippa?"

"Why now, sire? Why send a party at all? I think it means the enchantment is weakening, and if so, we can break it."

"Perhaps, but we are back where we started. Do *you* know how to break this enchantment? For, certainly, I do not."

She knelt and brushed the grit from her hands. It was dark enough that if her fingertips were stained purple, she couldn't tell. Her lips too, she supposed. But perhaps *that* wasn't such a bad thing.

"I have a notion, if you'll allow me."

"Allow you what, Lady Pippa?"

"A liberty."

Although he remained seated, Prince Bennett straightened, adjusted his tunic. "Very well, then. Take your liberty." He spread his arms wide. "I am at your disposal."

Yes, he was making fun of her. But what if it worked?

She crept forward, closer to the prince. The moment her face brushed the stardust that surrounded him, the enchantment shimmered across her skin. Once she was inside the halo, she heard its hum. This was some strong magic. Even so, this one small gesture might break it. If nothing else, this one small gesture felt right.

She leaned forward, chin tilted upward so she might look the prince in the eye. His gaze was dark, unfathomable. He held himself absolutely still except for the barest nod of his head.

She kissed him then, eyelids fluttering closed, the hum of the enchantment roaring in her ears. There was a spark when their lips touched, and a sweetness swept through her.

For one moment, everything vanished. There was no forest, no kingdom, no conniving brother, no cruel hunting party. There was only the two of them, alone. There was strong magic in this, too. It thrummed through the night, filled her with hope and unexpected longing.

Pippa sat back and pressed her palms against her thighs, anxious to see the results of such strong magic. In the wake of their kiss, the bear-shaped halo was still sparkling around Prince Bennett. The enchantment shimmered and hummed exactly as it had before.

Nothing had changed. Certainly the magic had been strong enough, and she'd been so certain it would work.

She heaved a sigh of discouragement. "That was disappointing."

"Well, I have been a bear for nearly a year. You'll forgive me if I'm out of practice."

She frowned, not understanding his meaning. Then the force of it—of what she'd said—struck her. Heat bloomed in her cheeks. She opened her mouth to apologize, but he was already laughing.

His body shook with it. He threw his head back, gulped a breath, and took up laughing again. It went on for so long that if he hadn't been the heir to the throne, she would've considered cuffing him on the side of the head.

At last, he held up a hand as if in apology. "Gods and stars," he murmured. "I have not laughed so much or felt so ... human in nearly a year." He regarded her then. With only a sliver of the moon in the night sky, she couldn't read his expression. "Perhaps even more than a year."

She wanted to ask what he meant, but her face was burning too hot, and she didn't trust her mouth—not when it had betrayed her several times already today.

"You gave it a valiant try, Lady Pippa, but I'm afraid it will take more to break this enchantment. Certainly my brother has considered that."

Certainly he had. And despite her mortification, she found her voice. "I still say something is different, sire, and I think you—"

"Should take advantage of that. Agreed. But not now. Now, you need a few hours of rest before we make the journey back to the palace. If we time it right, you'll be back in your quarters before sunrise."

"For all the good it will do me. I'd be better off venturing farther into the forest. Perhaps I could become a hermit."

Or reside in the cottage. Those weren't words she dared give voice to.

"Whatever for?"

"Begging your pardon, Your Highness, but have you seen my hair?" She ran her fingers through the curls, marveling once again at how short they were. "My mother will be beside herself. She won't be able to arrange a favorable match, not when I look like this. Truthfully, she won't be able to arrange an unfavorable one."

"You might be surprised." He raised a hand and leaned forward. "Allow me?"

She nodded, her breath catching in her throat.

His hands were strong, the fingers long and elegant and surprisingly gentle. He swept the curls from her forehead, tested the length of the strands, tilted his head and seemed to take in all of her.

"I think you look rather fetching. It suits you. Indeed, I prefer your hair this way."

Pippa opened her mouth to respond, then bit back her words. It would do no good to call the crown prince a liar. Besides, something told her he wasn't lying, not completely. He wasn't even sparing her feelings.

And as furious as her mother would be, Pippa couldn't find it in herself to truly miss the weight of her hair.

"You should rest now," he said, his hand gliding from her hair to her shoulder. "I'm afraid I can't offer you a fire. Even if I could light one, we shouldn't risk it."

"I'm warm enough."

"And if you stay by my side, we will both remain so."

His words held the hint of a question. Of course she'd remain by his side, where it was warm and smelled of blackberries. Only a ninny would clutch her skirts and scamper to the opposite end of the alcove.

Besides, Miven would never hurt her.

It was only as she drifted to sleep, curled against him, that Pippa remembered that Prince Bennett wasn't Miven, and Miven wasn't Prince Bennett.

But here, under the sliver of the moon, that didn't seem to matter.

CHAPTER 8

SHE WOKE ALL AT ONCE, the night black around her, a hand covering her mouth. The hand eased its grip until a single finger remained, pressed against her lips. Pippa nodded to show she understood.

For she could hear the crunch of underbrush, the crackle of twigs beneath boots. Behind her, Prince Bennett gripped her shoulders and helped her sit, the move silent and slow. Then his lips brushed her ear.

"They are very close," he said, his voice no louder than a whisper.

Pippa nodded.

"Do you remember where the pool is?"

She nodded again.

"On my mark, run there as fast as you can. I'll create a diversion and meet you on the opposite side, near the old willow."

That hand clamped over her mouth just as she was about to protest.

"It's dark," he said, as if he had anticipated what she might say. "My senses are far better than theirs and yours. I will find you, and then we'll run." He gripped her by the arms and then propelled her forward. "Now! Go!"

She did, clutching her skirt and crashing through the brambles. Shouts came from the woods. They echoed around her, the sound coming from all sides. Pippa scanned left and right, but the foliage was dense. Tree branches reached downward and grabbed the way a man might until she burst from their grasp. She stumbled forward, her heart thudding hard in her chest.

She reached the pool. Starlight shimmered against its surface, a mirror of the night sky. She scampered around its edge, careful not to splash and give herself away. The air here was still and serene.

Even so, something about the air was odd, and possibly too quiet, too peaceful. True, the hunting party was small. But if she'd been in charge, she would've left a man here to guard the most obvious escape route.

Pippa slowed her steps, and instead of dashing into the arms of the willow, she circumvented it. She hunkered down a few feet away and waited.

From the distance came the roar of a bear—and not just any bear. That was Miven's roar, fierce and loud, a proprietary roar, make no mistake. These were his woods, and the willow's branches quivered, and the ground trembled in response.

And then he was there, galloping through the pool on all fours, the spray of water like stars. He churned up the damp earth with sharp claws, but by the time he reached the willow, he was on two legs.

A strong hand, rather than a paw, clutched her own. He pulled her to her feet without breaking stride.

"We must run," he said.

She knew they should, that running was their only option. But something felt wrong about this side of the pool. If no sentry was stationed here, then what?

"I don't trust this. It feels too easy. It feels like a——"

"A trap. Yes. I know." He slowed, glanced back at her. "And yet, we don't have a choice."

It was the glance backward that saved him. Prince Bennett only slipped, rather than plunged, into a pit, one hidden by dry leaves spread across a delicate lattice of branches.

His hand jerked from her grip. She teetered on the edge of the pit, arms flailing for balance. He held on with one hand and used the claws of the other to gain purchase. Pippa caught herself, caught her breath, and then launched forward to keep him from sliding in completely. The stardust shimmered, and beneath her palms, she alternately felt fur and the prince's royal tunic.

"Run," he said through gritted teeth. "You must run. It's the only option. You can't save me, and I won't have them harming you."

"I'm not leaving you." Even as she said it, her arms began to ache. Both man and bear were far too heavy for her to tug to the surface. But if she could help, if her meager strength would allow him to gain purchase? Well, then, she'd offer it.

"Run, Lady Pippa. As your sovereign, I command you."

"You're a bear. You command no one."

She thought he might roar at that. Before he could, the shouts of men echoed through the woods.

"We got him! Tell the prince! We got him!"

The prince? As in Prince Beauregard? Pippa could feel her heart pound against the earth, and the taste of copper and sour soil filled her mouth. She gripped Prince Bennett tighter, but he'd gone still in her hands.

"So, it's come to this," he said.

And then he let go.

CHAPTER 9

A SOFT THUD and a grunt told her that Prince Bennett had landed. The pit, then, wasn't so deep. Not that she could pull him out, not even if they had all the time in creation. She rubbed her arms and wished them stronger than they were.

She crouched at the side of the pit and considered. What could she do on her own?

The thrashing in the woods grew louder. Certain of their quarry, the men were no longer bothering with stealth. That could work to her advantage. Or would if she could only concoct some sort of plan.

The earth beneath her palms felt clammy, stickier than it should be. She brushed her hands against her dress and then brought her fingertips to her face. Copper, again. Blood, then. That glimmer formed on the surface of the pit. She reached out, let her fingertips flow through the stardust, and witnessed the transaction in her mind's eye. The flash of a dagger across a royal palm.

A blood oath, one renewed, possibly made even stronger. What could they use to fight that?

The answer suggested itself almost as she thought the words. Those three drops of blood striking the forest floor. Miven's promise to her all those years ago:

My blood will protect you.

Would it? Was this what he'd meant?

The crashing in the woods grew louder still. Pippa surveyed the clearing, then the dark gap of the pit in front of her. There was no good place to hide ... unless ...

"Your Highness?"

Nothing but silence emerged from the dark hole.

"Sire, I know you can hear me. I'm coming down. I suggest you transform into Miven in order to catch me."

With that, Pippa swung her legs over the edge of the pit. She clutched at the earth, but the lower her legs went, the looser her grip became, until, at last, her fingers slid through the mud and clutched at nothing but air.

She fell, the pit swallowing her up before a black, furry embrace caught her. He was warm and solid, and the scent of blackberries mixed with those of earth and copper.

"I thought I told you to run," he began, the words starting as a growl and ending with royal indignation. He let her slip through his arms and land in a heap on the floor of the pit.

This was fine with Pippa. That put her at boot height, on a level with that dagger. He wasn't going to give that up willingly.

She didn't bother with stealth. There wasn't time.

Without finesse, she yanked the dagger from the sheath strapped to his calf and scampered away so he couldn't grab it back.

"Gods and stars, what are you—?"

"I won't let them kill you again." She raised the dagger, placing its tip at the top of the scar on her right arm. "My blood will protect you."

She plunged the blade into her flesh.

What felt like fire raced across her skin. The new wound ignited the old one. Her arm throbbed, and blood rushed downward, soaking her sleeve, her hand, dripping off her fingertips.

Prince Bennett caught her as her knees gave out. They sank to the ground, and when he went to cover the wound, she slapped his hand away.

"Blood ... to counter blood." She forced the words out between gasps.

The night flared to life. Torches lit the world over their heads. But even as the light illuminated the space above, the pit remained in blackness.

"It was right here," one of the men was saying. "We dug the pit right here. Look at the piles of dirt."

"Means nothing," a second man said.

"But I'm telling you—"

"Don't tell me. Tell Prince Beauregard."

Shouts echoed once again, the world above almost like day as more men and torches joined the gathering.

Then everyone fell so silent, Pippa swore she could hear the hiss of the torches burning.

"Am I to understand that the pit you dug earlier has mysteriously vanished?"

"Begging your pardon, Your Highness." The man's voice quavered until it cracked on the last word. "It was right here, and the bear ... The bear fell in. We trapped it. I swear to you."

A single pair of boots crunched the earth above them, then what looked like a shadow stretched across the pit. Only it was no shadow, but Prince Beauregard himself, standing above the pit, on what would be its center.

From her vantage point, Pippa could see the soles of his boots, a hint of gold braid on his tunic, the warm glow of velvet. It was if the prince were walking on glass.

He looked down, and she swore he stared straight at her. He tapped the toe of his boot once, twice, three times.

"Here, you say?" And his voice was as clear and cold as the finest crystal.

"Yes, Your Highness."

"I see. Why don't you show me where, exactly."

This was no suggestion, but a royal command, and the man shuffled forward. In the torchlight, his cheeks appeared yellow, his eyes huge and frightened.

The men above had her full attention, so when Prince Bennett captured her around the waist and pulled her toward the wall of the pit, she nearly cried out.

"Don't look," Prince Bennett whispered, and he gathered her closer as if they both could vanish into the earth. "That is all. Don't look."

She didn't, at least, not full-on. She didn't need to.

She heard the scrape of a sword being drawn, the sound of blade meeting flesh, the thud of a man dead before he hit the ground.

"Take this as a warning, gentlemen. I do not suffer fools—or incompetence—gladly. The next time we venture into these woods, I suggest you secure your quarry before alerting me."

Prince Beauregard stepped from view, to clean his sword, perhaps. For when Pippa next saw him, his blade was sheathed, and he stalked above their heads like a man who knew he was missing something crucial.

He tipped his head toward the sky, and Pippa could see the flash of pale neck. His sigh held frustration. "We are done here." He raised his chin as if tasting the air, or perhaps the magic in it. "Yes, we'll get no further tonight. Let us return to the palace."

But before he left, Prince Beauregard walked the circumference of the pit, his boots making nary a sound. He peered into its depths. What he saw, Pippa couldn't say, but she did know this:

He greeted that sight with a smile.

CHAPTER 10

THEY WAITED, their backs against the earth. Once the crickets started to chirp, and creatures rustled the underbrush, Prince Bennett sank to the ground, and Pippa, still in his grip, followed.

"I think," he said, his voice low, "that we can risk bandaging your arm."

Pippa nodded, and that one small movement made her head swim. She wavered back and forth and bumped his shoulder.

"You've lost a great deal of blood." He slipped from her and held her steady with one hand while the other patted his tunic. "I'm afraid I have nothing to use as a bandage."

"My chemise," she said. Only a hint of a flush heated her cheeks. She was too woozy, too relieved to care about whether the prince should see her chemise. "Tear a bit. It doesn't matter. It's all ruined anyway, but that's probably the cleanest."

"You sound less than devastated," the Prince observed.

"I don't care for gowns. If I could, I'd wear breeches, like a man."

"Hm. That would be..." He let the sentence trail off.

"What, sire?" Pippa prompted. "That would be what?"

"Practical, at the very least." Prince Bennett knelt and, with utmost care, eased the skirt of her dress just high enough that he could slice a strip from her chemise. Then he froze, knife in hand.

"I'm not certain I should risk this."

The dagger was steady and sure in his hand, but even so, Pippa could detect a hint of claw, a tuft of fur.

"As Miven?" she suggested.

He nodded once, although it was too dark to see if his expression held any chagrin. He sheathed the dagger, and with the utmost care, used a single claw to tear a strip from the bottom of her chemise.

"There," he said once the makeshift bandage was taut against the wound. "Can you stand?"

"I think so."

He helped Pippa to her feet. Her head still swam, and she swayed back and forth. He held her steady, a hand at her waist and one on her uninjured arm.

"I'm afraid I don't have a plan for getting us out, either," he said. "I might be able to claw my way up, but this trap was designed to defeat both a bear and a man."

"I see a way out," she said.

"Indeed?" he said, his voice full of skepticism and curiosity.

She pointed over his shoulder to where the branches of the weeping willow were weaving themselves into a ladder. The prince spun, confronted the sight, and then spun again to confront her.

"Gods and stars. You, Lady Pippa, are a witch. I'm certain of it."

His words were in jest, but she shook her head. "It's the blood. The earth is still damp with it."

And my blood will protect you.

Slowly, they clambered up the ladder. The branches trembled beneath their boots. Pippa's arm ached from shoulder to fingertips; it was useless, or nearly so, flopping at her side. The prince threw himself over the top and then reached down for her. He lifted her the rest of the way as if she weighed no more than a leaf.

Early morning birdsong greeted them—as did the sight of the dead man.

Prince Bennett knelt and closed the man's eyes. "A pity and a waste."

Her gaze darted—from the man, to the pit, to the pile of dirt left behind. Certainly they should fill the trap anyway, so no one else—human or animal—could fall in. "Perhaps we should—"

Before she could finish speaking, the dirt faded from view. The man vanished next, and Prince Bennett leaped back in surprise. He looked at her and then at the pit behind her.

Solid earth had filled the hole, and the ground was

unmarked by shovels and spades and even footprints. She tapped the space with the toe of her boot.

"I misspoke, Lady Pippa. Here is the true witchcraft."

"Do you think this man was meant as a ... sacrifice?" She spoke with caution, hesitation. It was one thing for the prince to accuse his brother of misdeeds, and quite another for her to do so.

"Perhaps I was not the intended target for this outing, merely an excuse."

"People say the magic has soured." She held out her hands as if she could touch some of that magic. "But I wonder if it's being misused. If you fed the woods such a thing"—she nodded to where the man had fallen —"would it grow ever hungrier?"

He didn't answer, and she knew—no matter the circumstances—that it truly was unwise to accuse his brother of such things.

It didn't stop her from wondering what Prince Beauregard might have done and what had happened to her woods in the past seven years.

"We should get you back to the palace," Prince Bennett said at last. "Before the sun rises."

"And before I'm asked questions I can't possibly answer."

The state of her dress. The wound on her arm. Her hair. How would she explain that? She couldn't hide from her mother forever. Despite all that, the only notion that squeezed her heart was that she must leave the woods behind her.

She studied the prince. The stardust outline was

sparkling in the early morning light. He was so like Miven; it wasn't simply the enchantment. He was strong and stalwart. He would rule the kingdom with a level head and a steady hand. He would not ... indulge the way his brother did.

But most of all, he was Miven returned to her.

"Come," he said, and held out his hand. "Let us get you home."

Pippa took his hand, and together they found the path that would lead her out of the woods. She didn't have the heart to tell him that her true home was in the other direction.

CHAPTER 11

"I CAN GO NO FARTHER."

They hid in the saplings and underbrush that bordered the meadowlands. In the distance, the pale stone of the castle was glowing pink with the rising sun.

"Do you sense it?" the prince asked. "I am more bear than man."

Yes, the outline of Miven did more than shimmer about him. It looked solid. If she reached out a hand, she might touch the soft fur. The warm scent of blackberries filled the pocket of space between them.

"If I leave these woods, I will become a bear forever."

Leaving these woods would break her heart forever. She sighed with so much force, the leaves in front of her face rattled.

Prince Bennett laughed, not the full-throated laugh of earlier, but a more muted chuckle.

"Is the prospect of a warm bath and a proper bed so distressing?"

It wasn't, of course, but she could no more explain her heartache to him than she could to herself.

"I should like to stay in the woods," was all she said.

"Well, you could return. To the cottage, that is. I'm afraid that if you don't, it will be nothing but crying and braying from Brindle."

She could ... return? "Do you mean that?"

"About Brindle? Yes. He is quite vocal."

She exhaled, not quite a laugh and not a sigh. "About my returning."

"Indeed, Lady Pippa. You ... belong there."

She studied not the man at her side or the woods behind her, but the castle. If she belonged in the cottage, then certainly Prince Bennett belonged on the throne.

"And if I arrived with better chatter than the squirrels might bring you?" she ventured.

"I wouldn't ask that of you."

"What if I'm offering my services?"

"Spying is a dangerous game, Lady Pippa. With my brother poised to rule, it is also a treasonable offense."

"Will he run me through with his sword?"

"Beauregard is capable of far worse, I'm afraid."

"And I'm afraid that if you don't return, things will be far worse for everyone in the kingdom."

He held her gaze, his coal-black eyes unfathomable. Then he waved a hand in defeat.

"Very well. Do as you wish. For I am merely a bear, and I command no one."

His words stole her breath, and the heat of shame burned her cheeks. She shifted to face him, stood, and then executed an awkward curtsy. "Forgive me, sire. I spoke rashly, and I only wished—"

"To save my life. Understood, Lady Pippa. There's no need for forgiveness. But trust me when I say it's unlikely I'll ever forget."

And there it was again, that almost-smile tugging at the corner of his mouth, and his dark eyes sparkled with what might have been humor.

"It's time," he said. "Make haste. Return when you can, but do not put yourself in danger to do so."

She raced into the meadow without looking back. Pippa knew if she did, she might not ever return to the castle. She'd be content to spend her days and nights in the cottage. It would be so simple, so easy, but ultimately, everyone else would suffer.

So she ran across the meadowlands, poppies swaying in her wake, and burst into the manicured gardens. Halfway to the castle, she thought to unwrap the cloth from around her arm. The blood was no longer flowing, but a few drops scattered as she ran.

My blood will protect you.

When she reached her chambers undetected, Pippa knew it had.

CHAPTER 12

PIPPA SCRUBBED the grime from her skin. A full bath would have to wait until later, but for now she was clean enough. She found an old chemise and tore strips to wrap her arm. She pulled on a dress with generous sleeves.

Only her hair confounded her. She stared at her reflection, tugging at her short curls as if that might lengthen the strands. A headdress, perhaps, but she'd never worn them, and a change of fashion might be noticed. If she was to spy for Prince Bennett, she'd need to be as unobtrusive as possible.

"What, then?"

Pippa said the words aloud, to the air, to the room around her, to the summer day outside her window.

It was then that a sparrow landed on the sill. It hopped through the open window and onto the floor. A second bird followed, then a third.

An entire flock fluttered through the window and swooped toward her dressing table.

She let out a cry and stumbled backward. Then she could only stare in amazement.

In a flurry of ribbons and feathers and golden strands, the birds fluttered back and forth. With claws and beaks, they wove an intricate pattern. Only when they had finished did she realize what they'd done.

They'd returned her shorn hair, every last strand, from the looks of it. Each of those strands was attached to the ribbon.

And she could tie that ribbon about her head. Her locks would cascade down her back like they always had.

"Oh! Thank you!"

The birds fluttered from her chambers, except for that first sparrow. It swooped down and dropped a leaf onto her dressing table before it, too, flew from the room.

On that leaf, in what looked like ink made from berry juice, were a few scrawled words:

I may command no one, but if this finds you, it means the birds, at least, will listen.

Pippa raced to the window. Her view of the forest was no more than pines and oaks merging into a hazy green. She certainly couldn't see the cottage. But she leaned out the window and whispered into the morning.

"Me, Your Highness. I will listen."

She waited there. When a breeze swept the curls from her face, Pippa could've sworn it carried the hint of laughter as a reply.

ABOUT THE AUTHOR

CHARITY TAHMASEB has slung corn on the cob for Green Giant and jumped out of airplanes (but not at the same time). She spent twelve years as a Girl Scout and six in the Army; that she wore a green uniform for both may not be a coincidence. These days, she writes fiction (long and short) and works as a technical writer for a software company in St. Paul.

ALSO BY CHARITY TAHMASEB

YOUNG ADULT FICTION (WITH DARCY VANCE)

The Geek Girl's Guide to Cheerleading

Dating on the Dork Side

YOUNG ADULT FICTION

The Fine Art of Keeping Quiet

The Fine Art of Holding Your Breath

Now and Later: Eight Young Adult Short Stories

FANTASY

Coffee and Ghosts, Season 1

Coffee and Ghosts, Season 2

Coffee and Ghosts, Season 3

www.ingramcontent.com/pod-product-compliance
Lightning Source LLC
Chambersburg PA
CBHW020614120726
47905CB00003B/785